GRYFFON
MASTER

CURSE OF THE
LICH KING

PROFESSOR K.R. LIMN
BOOKS

GIANT TALES:
Beyond the MYSTIC DOORS
From the MISTY SWAMP
World of Pirates
LAVA STORM

CRYSTAL SWORD CHRONICLES:
GRYFFON MASTER

CRYSTAL SWORD CHRONICLES

Gryffon

Master

CURSE OF THE
LICH KING

CHRISTIAN WARREN FREED
JOYCE SHAUGHNESSY
H.M. SCHULDT
RANDALL LEMON
LYNETTE WHITE

PROFESSOR K.R. LIMN BOOKS
writers750.com
Charlotte, North Carolina

Professor Limn Books may be purchased
for educational, business, or sales promotional use.
For information please write to: H. M. Schuldt
writers750.com

Cover Design © 2013 Northlake Art Studio

First published in 2013 by Professor Limn Books
ISBN 978-0-988578449

First Edition, December 2013

To Sara Otto

I'll forever be grateful
for your passion and ability,
for your thirst for literature, and
for your spirit of a warrior
to bring words to life.

Preface

Five authors
have come together
in a remarkable way
with one purpose:
to write a story about a
Viking and an Arab who briefly meet
under dangerous circumstances
in a strange jungle world
where living skeletons, trolls,
dragons, and other creatures roam free.
The two main characters in this book
are completely ficticious.
Ragnar Olafson
is a Northman Warrior
from Larvik, and
Ahmad Ibn Fazzat
is a Bedouin Soldier
from Damascus.

PROFESSOR K.R. LIMN

Contents

1. Jotun 1

2. Poisonous Stingers 4

3. A Slimy Lich 8

4. Swamp Troll 12

5. Grave Robbers 16

6. Crystal Chamber 21

7. Water Hole 25

8. Dragonfly Vision 30

9. A Beetle 34

10. Unexpected Visitors 38

11. Sand Battle 42

12. The Hut 46

13. Summoning 50

14. Horgoth's Secret 54

15. Chain Mail 60

16. The Prophesy 65

17. Trouble at Yggdrasil 69

18. City in the Sand 73

19. Sand Skimmer 77

20. The Third Human 82

21. Stranger in a Strange Land 87

22. Lizard Goblin 90

23. City of the Dead 95

24. Tombstone 101

25. A Rattling Voice 107

26. A Deadly Chill 111

27. Dragon Toe 115

28. Trapped in Mud 119

29. Delfin's Formula 123

30. Blinded 129

31. Angry Thunder 133

32. Potions 137

33. Haunted Canyon 142

34. Master Climber 147

35. Writing On the Wall 152

36. A Kingly Gift 158

37. A Soldier's Arrow 162

38. Darustrix Irthos 166

39. Barrel's Den 171

40. Twilight Breeze 178

Afterword

Christian Warren Freed

Joyce Shaughnessy

H.M. Schuldt

Randall Lemon

Lynette White

Introduction

In a place far away, there is a strange world of trolls and liches and other horrible monsters. Two adventurers have stumbled into this dangerous jungle—one is a Viking and the other is an Arab. Ragnar Olafson must find a way to escape while Ahmad Ibn Fazzat has literally been snatched from the jungle, but he must fulfill his destiny to return. Soon they learn about a great prophecy, one that requires both of them to put an end to a slimy Lich King. Ragnar encounters two of the most remarkable dvergar (dwarves), Karlo and Kerr, who are on the run from a wicked woman, Queen Valona, even though they are sent by the King to destroy a cursed necklace.

Many years earlier, an evil ruler named Traven the Fallen forced a young dvergr jeweler named Karagon to make a powerful necklace for Traven's wife, Thora. To stop Traven's reign of terror and his greedy quest to rule the land, two strangers from faraway lands were called upon to use a specially crafted crystal sword, which was supposed to destroy the necklace. The two strangers fought in a battle against Traven, but Thora stole the crystal sword. One night Karagon snuck in and was able to take back his necklace. After many years, this necklace ended up in the hands of Queen Valona. It brought trouble to the Dwarf Mine of Davlin, causing the undead spirit of Traven, the evil Vatman, to discover the necklace. So the King ordered Karlo to take it far away and destroy it.

A remarkable work from five authors, Gryffon Master brings you a creative story packed with action and thrills. No doubt it will lead to an incredible understanding that there is a warrior in all of us.

PROFESSOR K.R. LIMN

1

Jotun

by
Christian Warren Freed

"What is your name?"

He blinked rapidly. Head pounding and vision blurred, Ragnar vaguely recognized the sound of another human voice. Struggling to rise, he fell back—in pain and exhaustion.

"Relax and get your breath. You are experiencing the effects of the fall. I know this, for I too have felt it. I am Ahmad Ibn Fazzat, and I come from Damascus. Can you remember your name?"

A cough. Wracking pain in his ribs. "Ragnar Olafson. I am from Larvik. What is this place? I have never seen trees like this."

The jungle grew thick in all directions. Heavy underbrush choked the ground. Thin mists clung to the ground, unwilling to disappear back into the void. Plants and trees neither man had ever seen closed in around them, confining their world to mere meters. The air was thick with moisture. Strange animal sounds mocked them from the distance.

Ahmad nodded. He couldn't help but notice the distinct differences in their appearances. Ragnar had pale skin with bleached golden locks of unkempt hair. His clothing was poor quality, mostly animal skin. Strange markings tattooed his face and arms. Everything about him suggested a caged predator.

"I do not know. I was part of a caravan heading to the siege of Jerusalem when there was a blinding light, greater than the sun. When I awoke I was alone and here. This is not natural."

Ragnar rubbed his aching chest, jangling his necklace of bones. "Our boat had just landed in Frisia to raid. The light claimed me as well. I was certain Hel had come to claim me."

Ahmad helped Ragnar stand. The Northman leaned heavily on Ahmad while he recovered his strength.

"Once you are healthy we should try to find a way out of this," Ahmad suggested. "So unlike my home. We have trees and gardens worthy of praise but nothing like this. We have sand as far as the eye can see, and it is very dry and hot. I do not like this place."

Ragnar nodded. "I come from tall mountains covered with snow most of the year. The sea is my home as much as any building. I can stand on my own now, Ahmad."

Ahmad tossed his riding cloak over his shoulders and gestured. "The sun is heading in this direction. I suggest we track it. Perhaps we will discover the answers we need to escape."

They walked for hours—the sun never going down. The jungle thickened, offering no freedom. Both felt confined and became desperate to be under the open sky again. Much later they arrived at an odd clearing. Nothing grew for ten meters, all a perfect circle. A beam of sunlight stabbed down in the center, and their eyes were magnetically drawn. A crystal sword lay across a large tree stump. Light reflected rainbows off the weapon.

Ragnar noticed Ahmad had no weapon and, despite a growing desire to possess the sword, he said, "Take it. I have my axe. My heart tells me we shall have need of as many weapons as possible before this madness has passed."

Hesitant to break the circle of light, Ahmad licked his lips and took the first step. He whispered a prayer and gently reached down. The moment his fingers touched the sword, a blood-curdling roar erupted from the jungle.

Ahmad snapped up at the unexpected sound. Cold shivers bled down his spine, so alien and foreign was the scream. The ground trembled under heavy footsteps from an impossible creature. "What devil is this?"

"Jotun!" Ragnar bellowed and hefted his axe. "We must flee!"

Trees exploded, ripped into the air like massive spears. Frost crept ahead of the giant's advance. Snow and arctic winds howled through the trees. They heard the frost giant's howl. It was close. Ragnar raced forward and grabbed Ahmad by the collar. Ahmad had enough wits to grab the sword, and they ran for their lives.

2

Poisonous Stingers

by
Joyce Shaughnessy

Ragnar yelled over the roar of the mighty Jotun, a frost giant, "Keep running! He has many powers! We must run!"

Ragnar and Ahmad ran until they could no longer move their legs. The jungle seemed to encroach upon them with every move, the leaves and vines encircling their feet.

Ragnar, sensing that Ahmad was about to fall, suggested they stop and rest.

The two men tried to settle the breathing in their chests. Ahmad asked Ragnar, "Who is Jotun?"

"They are frost giants who inhabit our world in the coldest part of the cosmos, the Jotunheimr. If we tarry too long, he will lure us to sleep with his magical powers, and we will go to the afterlife. I would rather die in battle and be taken to Valhalla, not beaten by a monster and end up in Hel."

Each man assessed the other. Ragnar was not impressed by Ahmad. He was small and wiry. "You do not belong to my world. How is it you speak my tongue?"

Ahmad answered, "I speak many languages. I have seen many different worlds in my travels but nothing as strange as this place." The air choked his breath as he spoke.

"How is it a frost giant can inhabit a jungle such as this?"

"I know not how. We must be caught in a cosmos between worlds. The sword—it didn't burn your hand when you grabbed it. I felt sure it would. It was glowing with such intensity."

"No," Ahmad answered. "It is magnificent. I think it is the jewels that make it glow. I don't know how useful it would be in battle. Perhaps it possesses special powers. I can no longer hear the roar of the giant. Perhaps we escaped him. Maybe he cannot live in the jungle." He paused and said, "I'm not certain that we can for very long. We must continue our journey. This is not the way I intend to die. We have to find water. It is odd, but the air is so thick it makes me feel more thirst than the desert."

It seemed as if Ahmad needed only request it—a large waterfall suddenly appeared before them.

Their thirst quenched, the two men crept forward with obvious trepidation, not knowing what strange creatures or world they might encounter.

Ragnar whispered, "This is indeed a strange cosmos where we find ourselves."

Suddenly the jungle cleared and from the sky, an enormous gryffon appeared! He was majestic as he swooped over the clearing and settled on a boulder a small distance away from the two men. His intelligent eyes held a strength and knowledge of the ages. The gryffon's mighty wings spanned many feet and beat with such mightiness that he stirred the air into a strong wind. His eyes seemed to be judging each man as his forceful talons gripped the massive boulder. The muscles in his forelegs tensed as if he were about to leap forward.

Ragnar fell to his knees in awe and respect for the mighty beast. He had only heard tales of such a creature.

In a swoop so graceful and swift that neither man saw him rise, the gryffon raised his enormous wings and flew over them. He picked up Ahmad with his strong talons and rose into the air over the forest, leaving Ragnar on his knees. Ahmad dangled helplessly from the talons of the huge gryffon. He wished that he could climb on the gryffon's large back so that he could ride him like he would a horse. He looked down as Ragnar slowly dimmed from view.

Ragnar looked in the sky, hoping that Ahmad would appear again, but he disappeared quickly, leaving him alone in the strange world. Ragnar crept forward and soon found himself in a thick forest much like before. The air was thick and damp, but he carried on.

Ragnar prayed that he would find the sea and his boat again. He swung his axe beside his strong legs as they carried him deeper into the jungle, deeper into the unknown. He walked for many hours, but Ragnar's body was young and strong. He reminded himself that he was Ragnar Olafson, a descendent of the mighty god, Odin. He imagined how Odin would have reacted had he been thrown into this strange world with mysterious creatures. He knew instantly that Odin would have fought until he could no longer breathe, and he would seek the knowledge required to exist here.

Ragnar felt something crawling on his legs, both legs at once. He looked down and saw huge scorpions on his thick breeches! He could only use the handle of the axe against them. As Ragnar fought to free himself from the huge stingers, he could see their enormous tails curling upward, ready to strike! He suspected that if they reached his arms and these enormous insects stung him, the poison would kill him!

As if from the earth itself, a dvergr, or dwarf appeared! He quickly brushed the stingers from Ragnar's legs and in minutes had pounded them into the earth with a large stone. After dispatching them to the grave, the dvergr stood before Ragnar and waited for his due respect.

3

𝔄 𝔖𝔩𝔦𝔪𝔶 𝔏𝔦𝔠𝔥

by
H. M. Schuldt

Kerr, the first pale skinned dvergr, smashed two scorpions and dropped the stone. Ragnar turned around when he heard a purring sound. He saw another huge scorpion scuttle away as Karlo, the second dvergr, the taller one of the two, came running into the area. The scorpion crawled next to a rock while Karlo took out a large empty pouch from under his cloak. The rattle started again as Karlo slowly approached the twelve-inch killer to make a capture.

"I smashed two crawlers, Karlo," young Kerr acknowledged.

"Your smashing saved the furry man's life. I need to capture this crawler for its venom," Karlo answered.

Bending low Karlo moved closer to the venomous invertebrate. He knew about the killer's poor eyesight. His training days in the Dwarf Mine of Davlin had paid off. He came around from the side, swooped up the deadly crawler, and placed it in his cloth bag. The rattle stopped. He tied the pouch shut and tossed it off to the side.

Ragnar spoke sarcastically under his breath as he was still recovering from two scorpions that had just clung to his legs. He rejected how it almost frightened him. "How the young peccary would grunt if he knew how the old boar suffers."

"The what? Have no fear. I'll take it with us when we go," Karlo assured, glancing at the bag. "Blasted sun! I'm more worried about getting sunshine on my skin than a few scorpions."

"I owe you my finest gratitude. I've heard about scorpions, but this is the first time I've seen one." Ragnar said, shaking Kerr's thick dwarf hand. "At least I didn't fall into a pit of vipers. I'm Ragnar Olafson from the North. Do you know the way back to Larvik? Have you heard of Larvik?"

"Where?" Kerr asked. "No, my friend. We spend all our time in the Dwarf Mine of Davlin beyond the Mossy Rock. We only came out to go to the boneyard and…"

"And to collect some rosy periwinkle," Karlo interrupted. "Let me introduce myself. I'm Karlo, the son of Reginn, from the tribe of Valinn. This is my Tyro, Kerr, my young apprentice. Nice set of bones you got there." He wiped his palm on his dark cloak and held out his workman hand for a proper introduction.

It came as no surprise that Ragnar felt an instant friendship develop. Two black haired dvergar had saved his life. Back where he had come from, Ragnar did everything he could to give recognition where it was due. On the battlefield, he had seen remarkable heroic deeds as well as other strange things. This was the first time he saw anyone battle a large scorpion. He accepted that Kerr had come to his rescue out of the goodness in his heart. But as the conversation continued, it seemed as if this heroic deed had to be kept a secret when they returned to the mines because black Emperor scorpions were prized for defense and medical use. Ragnar found it quite odd that Karlo held the scorpion in high regard. Still, he went along with the informative discussion.

"Karlo, he might know something about it," Kerr nudged.

Karlo saw that Kerr was pushing him to show Ragnar a particular necklace, but the older dwarf paused to consider the consequences. Karlo was carrying this valuable necklace, yet he had been ordered to destroy it.

The necklace debate of whether or not they should show it to Ragnar continued for some time until Karlo finally agreed to show it to Ragnar. He reached into his dark flowing cloak and pulled out a small coin pouch. Inside was a piece of jewelry very delicate for hammering hands to hold, but Karlo managed to hold up the golden necklace. It sparkled with red, green, and blue precious stones from an unknown place.

The discovery of the necklace in the Dwarf Mine of Davlin caused a great concern as to where it was made and whom it belonged to. It had the remarkable workmanship beyond anything ever found by a dvergr from Davlin. It was so magnificent for any eye to behold that the dwarf queen, Valona, became obsessed with it. Finally the dwarf king, Andren, took a drink of spiced grog and ordered Karlo to get rid of the cursed necklace. King Andren knew that it brought danger into the Dwarf Mine of Davlin. Queen Valona called for ten warriors to hunt down Karlo in order to take possession of the rare stones.

"We have necklaces like this where I'm from, but not many." Ragnar examined the fine piece of jewelry and read the inscription:

THORA

Karlo went on to describe the development of tomb building in the rocks of Davlin. Dark haired dwarves had engineered an underground tomb so extensive that it was easy to get lost unless a map was used. Even when a map was used, the clever dwarf king of Davlin frequently shut passages as a way to trap grave robbers.

Just when Ragnar was going to ask about where the necklace was found, they heard a terrible voice from beyond death.

"Give back the necklace." A male voice moaned from within a dark slimy skull.

The three men looked and saw a creepy skeleton with his left arm raised, his thin finger pointing at them. Weapons and strange pieces of metal hung from his arms and chest. He was draped from top to bottom in unusual flowing fur that hung directly from his bones. He did not move any further, but the lean creature held a long sword in his other boney hand. He was a Vatman from the Sunken Tomb of Vatomandry.

"A boneyard lich! Someone stole the necklace from a boneyard!" yelled Kerr. "Run!"

Karlo shoved the necklace back in his coin pouch, grabbed the scorpion, and took off. Kerr and Ragnar followed closely behind.

4

Swamp Troll

by

Randall Lemon

Fearing the evil Lich, the three sped on crashing through dense jungle growth. As much as he feared the undead sorcerer behind them, Ragnar realized he would have to slacken his pace or he would soon outdistance his shorter-legged companions.

All the while he ran, Ragnar's mind was spinning with possibilities. The dvergr had obviously seen a lich before and knew it for what it was. In his world, Ragnar knew Liches were drawn to sources of magic. Once they obtained these items, they would manipulate the energy contained in them to prolong their undead existence.

The lich appeared immediately after Karlo showed him the necklace and obviously desired to possess it. It appeared to Ragnar that they had probably discovered the jewelry while excavating the tomb of which they had spoken. Perhaps the lich had at one time possessed this necklace, and the dvergr had inadvertently stolen it from his underground lair?

Even though liches drain magic from powerful items leaving them useless, the one item a lich prized was its soul gem. This gem contained the essence of the lich itself. If the gem was destroyed, the lich would die forever. Could one of the gems on the necklace be the soul gem of this lich? If so, the monster would never give up trying to get it back.

The dvergr could run no further and had to rest. While they lay there gasping, Ragnar turned to Karlo. "Show me that necklace again. Something about it has been nagging at my brain."

Karlo nodded and reluctantly handed it over to Ragnar. He held it up turning it to catch the light. Suddenly it struck him! The color of the gems appeared in exactly the same pattern as the gems on the sword that he and Ahmad had found. This could not be a coincidence. Right after finding the sword, what they had desired most, water, magically appeared.

There was great magic afoot here. If only Ahmad were here with the sword, perhaps they could figure out the connection. In the time they had known each other, Ragnar had been impressed with the cleverness of his friend. Ahmad might be able to piece it out.

The dvergr appeared to have recovered. Ragnar got to his feet, "Karlo, are there any beings who live here who have knowledge of magic? I believe one of the stones on this necklace may possess great magic that belongs to that Lich. It might have worked to corrupt the soul of your queen changing her into the avaricious harridan you described. We need someone's aid in discovering a way to destroy this evil gem."

The two conferred for a moment, then turned to Ragnar, "There is a tribe of Swamp Trolls that live within a few hours from this spot. Unlike many of their evil ilk, this tribe is peaceful. They are led by an ancient shaman, a troll of great wisdom. If anyone can help us, we believe he can. We can lead you to him."

The threesome spent the next few hours wading through the thick jungle and looking over their shoulders fearing the evil being that was certainly following them seeking to recover the necklace. The dvergr moved into a swampy area following a brackish stream, which led them to the village of the Swamp Trolls.

When Ragnar spotted these trolls, he was surprised. The trolls of his frozen homeland were huge strapping beasts. By comparison, these trolls seemed to be under eight feet and so scrawny that Ragnar could count their ribs. Neither did the trolls rush to the attack when the three appeared at the edge of their village. Instead, there were warm greetings called out to the dvergr. Karlo led Ragnar to the largest hut in the village and before they could even announce their presence, a female troll pulled back the hide that covered the doorway and beckoned them in.

Ragnar walked into the hut and sat on the ground opposite an extremely old troll. Despite his age, this troll's eyes gleamed with intelligence. "I am Ahrns-Skra-Kae-Tung, Shaman of my tribe. I welcome my friends, Karlo and Kerr to my hut. And you are the furry man of my visions. For three nights, I have seen you in my dreams and I am unclear whether you bring fortune or destruction to my people. I know that evil follows you three. I have seen in my dreams that the furry man has another companion—one born of sand—while the furry man is born of ice! Somehow the Sandman flies while the furry man must walk but they are inextricably linked. Tell me why this evil follows you and why you come to Ahrns-Skra-Kae-Tung?"

The three took turns relating their stories. When they were done the shaman took some bones and colored stones from a basket, shook them, and cast them on the reed mat in front of him. He studied the pattern of their falling. "The future is never a certain thing. I tell you this much. You will need to find your friend, the Sandman. The sword you described is the only thing that can be used to destroy the soul gem. Without that sword you can never exterminate this lich who seeks you even now. If he should find you before you can regain the sword, and if you find which of the stones is the soul gem and seek to destroy it, he will try to catch you, suck the souls from your bodies, and turn you into mindless Undead who must serve him for eternity. What you must seek, furry man, lies far from here. I will give you a map of its general location. Once you get there, you will have to find its exact hiding place.

"What you need is a summoning stone that sits in a hidden treasure chest. When you find the chest, take only the summoning stone and rebury the rest of the treasure. Take the stone and keep it next to your heart for one full day. Then draw it forth and clutch it to your forehead and concentrate on images of the gryffon and your friend. Let nothing else enter your thoughts or break your concentration. If all goes well, your friend and the gryffon should be drawn inexorably toward your location. Then you may do what you must."

Ragnar studied the map that the old shaman had given them as Karlo toyed with the other gift the Troll had bestowed upon them; a small wooden triangle trinket around his neck. The trinkets had odd symbols carefully burned into the center and two intricately cut holes made it possible to attach it to a leather lacing.

5

Grave Robbers

by
Lynette White

Ahrns-Skra-Kae-Tung had told them the runes would only keep the lich at bay for three cycles of the sun, so it was crucial to complete their quest before the rune's power was spent. Judging the distance they had to cover, Ragnar found little comfort in that. His thoughts drifted to Ahmad as he wished he was the one on the gryffon now. Why did the gryffon carry Ahmad off, and where did he take his new found friend?

Ragnar forced himself to focus as he glanced at Karlo. His eyes moved to the necklace around Karlo's neck, and his hand moved to the identical one around his own. His eyes went back to the map as the pieces fell into place.

"Blessed Odin," he whispered, "a perfect triangle."

Karlo and Kerr traded apprehensive expressions.

"What is?" Kerr pressed.

Ragnar held up the map and pointed to the place where the necklace was found. Then he pointed to the place where the sword was found. And finally he pointed to the place where the summoning stone was believed to be. "These places form a perfect triangle. I find it hard to believe this is a mistake."

Karlo cleared his throat and looked at the ground. "It is not a mistake anymore than it is a coincidence we were all brought together."

He looked up at Ragnar. "I suspect the blood of the members in the original story flows in our veins. We are just the next chapter."

Karlo pointed at himself and Kerr. "Our blood is the same blood as the dvergr who was forced to craft this enchanted necklace. And now we have been commissioned to destroy it."

His finger moved to Ragnar. "The Gryffon Master from a far away land was entrusted with the sacred summoning stone. And a dark stranger from a different land was given the crystal sword. Together, they accepted the quest to destroy the necklace and the sorcerer.

"They did destroy the sorcerer, or at least his physical body, but they failed to destroy the necklace. So now we must finish what they started."

Ragnar threw up his hands in frustration. "What kind of insane world is this? I am not the descendant of some Gryffon Master! I have no purpose here."

"Perhaps you just never knew the truth about your bloodline." Kerr offered.

"Are you saying I don't know my heritage?" Ragnar challenged.

Karlo's eyes moved to his feet. "Not your heritage, Ragnar." He corrected him and looked up. "Your destiny." He paused. "Each of us has a role to play."

* * *

Night finally plunged the jungle into an impossible darkness. Ragnar tried to sleep, but the odd sounds from unseen animals and Karlo's words kept him awake.

Their quest resumed shortly after sunrise, and they traveled for hours before the jungle gave way to rolling hills and the mountain. The dvergar located a small cave opening into a massive cavern. The ceiling was hidden in darkness, and though Karlo lit a torch, they could only see just a little past their boots. Ragnar could not shake the overwhelming oppression he felt in this place.

He was about to succumb to the anxiety and flee when Karlo announced they had found the tomb. Ragnar stood beside Karlo and stared down at the open tomb at his feet. It had been excavated to the depth equivalent to Ragnar's knees. Pieces of broken statues and pottery littered the gravesite.

"Cursed grave robbers. What a mess!" Karlo growled and jumped into the open tomb.

"Isn't the person who found this cursed necklace a grave robber? And aren't we, at this very moment, doing the very same thing?" Kerr pointed out and jumped in after Karlo.

Ragnar hesitated. This was all wrong. He had no idea what he expected to find here but he took a deep breath and jumped into the tomb.

They were picking their way through the opened grave when Kerr found an ornate skeleton key. They made their way to a far corner and found it was left undisturbed. Karlo carefully started digging through the dirt. Before long his finger hit something hard. With a new found eagerness, they dug until they uncovered an ornately decorated wooden box that was still in remarkable condition. It was large enough to comfortably accommodate a small child. Karlo held the torch as Ragnar studied the designs on the lid.

The words engraved on the lid were written in some sort of strange language, but three symbols were conspicuous, a sword, a necklace, and a stone. Three different people, each resembling humans, held one of these items. The humans with the sword and the necklace stood opposite of each other while the third stood a short distance off beside a magnificent gryffon.

Ragnar did not have to read the strange language to guess the story that was being told. He moved to examine the hinges and the lock. They looked ancient but were somehow still in remarkable condition.

He pointed at the odd lock. "Do you know how to open this?"

Karlo smiled and nodded as he reached into a pocket of his cloak. He presented a small pouch and tugged on the strings. He searched through a variety of picks until he found the one he wanted. It did not take him long to get past the lock.

They held their breath as Ragnar opened the box. Several items were carefully placed inside including a second smaller box. Ragnar's mind flashed to the Shaman's warning so he used only his eyes to survey the contents. His eyes kept going back to the box. There was a familiarity about it that beckoned his attention.

He carefully picked up the box and examined it more closely. It, too, was locked.

"Kerr give me that key you found, please."

Kerr handed him the key, and Ragnar slipped it into the lock. The torch suddenly went out, and their lungs refused to accept air that reeked of evil. All eyes moved together to the red orbs floating a short distance away.

"You dare desecrate my resting place, take what is mine, and now you seek to gather my enemies?" The horrible voice of the lich echoed around them.

The three men simultaneously reached for the trinkets around their necks. Ragnar knew at that moment he had found what he was looking for. He also knew the lich could not harm them for another two days.

"It seems that way." He answered as his lips formed a smug grin.

6

Crystal Chamber

by

Christian Warren Freed

"We should leave this place, now, before it is too late," Karlo hissed. His knees trembled slightly.

Ragnar hefted his axe. Anger flashed across his face, darkening his features with latent fury. He was tired. Ever since waking up he'd been thrown into one bizarre situation after the next, and none of them made any sense. He desperately wanted to go back to sleep and awaken in his homeland again. To feel the cool autumn breeze come down from the snow covered mountains to kiss his flesh. To sing the songs of his forbearers and their great deeds. To drink to the All Father and pray for his place in the halls of Valhalla. That was Ragnar's life, not this macabre adventure.

Opening his eyes, Ragnar snorted and spat. "Let this foul creature come. My axe has not tasted blood in too long."

Kerr reached up to place a hand on Ragnar's forearm in caution. "No, Ragnar. We do not have the weapons to defeat this lich."

Ragnar stood ready for a challenge. "No. We push forward. This demon cannot harm us for the moment. We attack while the advantage is still ours."

Karlo and Kerr, reluctant to fight the impossible, stood with Ragnar lest he meet his doom alone.

* * *

Ahmad stared out the window from his lofty tower, silently taking in the breathtaking views of the land far below. Mountains capped in purple light jutted like broken teeth to the east. The gentle azure waters of an inland sea beckoned him to the north. And the jungle, foul and cloistering, mocked him from the south. But it was the west that grabbed his attention. Darkness clung there, blocking his vision and filling his heart with quiet dread. What madness lurks within? Can it possibly be worse than the giant?

"The view is not one normally afforded to outlanders," a soft voice said.

Ahmad turned to see a slender woman with golden skin float into the chamber. Long blonde hair flowed down past her shoulders. The diaphanous shift she wore echoed the colors of morning. Ornate pieces of jewelry covered her exposed flesh. She was the vision of a goddess.

"I am Faella, and I am a light elemental," she replied with a soft smile. "It was no mere accident that brought our paths together. You have a great destiny ahead of you, Ahmad Ibn Fazzat."

He held out his empty hands. "I am just a man. There is nothing special about me."

Faella's laugh tugged at his heart. "But you are. Our lands suffer from a curse. A blight cast upon us by a dying sorcerer's final whim. Two of you were brought here."

"Ragnar," Ahmad whispered.

"Yes. Already he goes to combat the darkness, but you must go down another path. Come with me, Ahmad," she beckoned.

He followed unquestioningly. Down the winding staircase and into the heart of the castle at the top of the world. The majesty of it flowed through Faella. So much so she appeared to float inches above the ground. Ahmad hadn't noticed it before. Questions entered his mind, but he dared not ask lest the moment was ruined.

They entered a crystal chamber. Rainbows of light reflected blinding him. Ahmad threw up an arm to protect his vision while Faella went to the center of the chamber. "This is the mirror of souls—a window to the deepest parts of mind and heart. Here you shall find the answers you seek and purpose will be delivered."

"I see yet suddenly find myself afraid," Ahmad replied.

Faella smiled sympathetically. "The mirror shows only what lies within your heart of hearts. Do you fear yourself?"

"No," he shook his head. Taking a deep breath, Ahmad opened his eyes.

Warm power flowed into his veins. He saw past and future—death and rebirth. Life blossomed, wilted, and faded to dull brown. The vision was so strong, it drove him to his knees. Tears flowed freely. He wept and stretched his hands to the skies. His mind trembled. Incredible pain invaded him and darkness claimed him.

When he awoke the chamber was dark. All of the earlier brilliance gone. Faella stood over him, watching him curiously. She had seen what he did and knew the truth of what was to come. Faella stretched out her hand and helped him to his feet. She passed a small vial as she did so.

"The future is clear but will not be pleasant," she said. "You walk a dangerous road, Ahmad Ibn Fazzat."

"It is not one I choose to take."

"But you must. The choice is no longer yours. Take this potion. It will give you strength when your courage fades. The gryffon is waiting to take you on your next journey. Take heart, Ahmad. Darkness will creep upon you, but all is not doom. You are the hope of us all."

Ahmad gave a final look back into the mirror of souls. "Ragnar, I am coming for you."

7

Water Hole

by
Joyce Shaughnessy

Darkness enfolded all three of the unlikely companions and threatened their doom even further. But for the present, it was impossible for the lich to penetrate into the circle of protection.

"Wait! Wait, Ragnar!" yelled Karlo. "First we must return to the treasure. Our duty is to leave everything *except the summoning stone*. Remember what the Shaman told us: You have to place the stone close to your heart for a full day."

Although Ragnar hated to leave a good fight to retrieve a stone, he knew Karlo was right. They quickly began digging through the treasure until Ragnar found the one that was vibrating with warmth.

"This is it!" Ragnar said.

Now they possessed what was needed to bring Ahmad back to this world.

Ragnar took the red stone and put it inside the folds of his clothing so that it rested on his heart, where it would stay for a full day. Since another night was drawing nigh, he knew the three must make as much progress that day as possible.

As Ragnar strode purposely out of the tomb and into the enormous cavern, he was struck again by the strangeness of this world. He yearned to stand among sunlight shining through the tall trees of his homeland. He softly whispered a prayer to Odin, "Please, dear Father, send me a sign! With your everlasting knowledge, I will do battle honorably and be victorious! Show me the way to go home."

He saw nothing. Then a small amount of sunlight managed to shine through the darkness. It came from the west, meaning that the day was fading. West was the direction they were headed, so the sunlight worked as something they could follow. Again, the strangeness mocked him.

How do creatures exist in this darkness?

Ragnar could hear the mumblings of the dvergar behind him as they argued about the correct direction to follow. Ragnar straightened his broad shoulders, swung his axe over his shoulder and for reassurance, felt the quiver strapped on his back—it held his arrows. The bow was strapped to the quiver with rope.

At least I am ready for battle.

Soon the three came upon a fork in the path. Ragnar asked aloud, "How do I know which fork will lead us on the right path?"

As they stood pondering his question, Ragnar heard the cawing of a crow coming from the right. Through the dimming sunlight he saw the black crow sitting on a branch. There was a small circle of sunlight shining on the crow's black eyes. Its eyes looked directly at Ragnar and back down the path to the right. It cawed loudly this time. Ragnar knew instantly that the crow was sent by Odin. It was the good omen for which he had prayed. The crow was a symbol of the great solar god, Godlug. If they followed the path to the right, they would either be victorious in battle or brave in death and be taken to the halls of Valhalla. Either way, the correct path was to the right.

Ragnar turned around to face Karlo and Kerr and said with a satisfied grin, "It is sign from my Father, Odin. Follow me!"

***

After safely securing the vitality potion in a pouch around his waist, Ahmad said to the beautiful Faella, "Thank you for your help. I wish I didn't have to leave this wondrous place, but I know that I must do my duty. How do I beckon the gryffon?"

She answered, "Just walk toward the window and ask for him to come and he will come to you. He is waiting for you."

Ahmad did as he was told, and he felt a strange sensation in his body. It was as if his entire form was being lifted up into the air. He closed his eyes as the feeling overtook him. Then he heard the heavy beating of gigantic wings as they stirred the air around him.

Ahmad heard a friendly sounding voice say, "Come with us, Ahmad Ibn Fazzat. My gryffon and I await you."

He turned his head and saw a gigantic creature before him. Riding him was someone he instinctively felt he could trust. The man was bathed in light and dressed in blue clothing that, in his Persian culture, indicated the color of immortality.

The man on the gryffon held out his left hand to lift Ahmad onto the gryffon so that he could sit behind him.

"My name is Simurgh, and I am the gryffon's master. I have been looking for him. He flew away from me in order to rescue you and bring you to our world. You must carry something magical with you. Otherwise, my gryffon, Rostok, would never have left me. He never leaves my side."

Ahmad answered, "It is the sword I am carrying. The first time I saw it, I wondered what strange powers it possessed. Then puzzling things started to happen. I wished for water, and a waterfall appeared. I wished to leave the strange cosmos where I had found myself, and Rostok stood before me. He picked me up and brought me to this beautiful place."

"But you have bidden Rostok again. You must need his further assistance."

"My friend, Ragnar, is still in the frightening world which I left. I'm afraid he needs our help. If we don't go to him, he will certainly die."

Simurgh nodded and said, "Then we must go. Rostok will take us there."

***

As the three travelers made their way through the deepening darkness, they suddenly saw ahead of them a wondrous water hole. It was steaming with heat and the warmth and presence beckoned them to rest beside it. Ragnar knew that night was definitely falling and they may as well rest by the water hole.

A strange light emanated from the steaming hole. Ragnar was somewhat overcome with the heat. In his home, all they had ever found was cold water from the sea and a few lakes which dotted the countryside. In his travels he had heard of lands where there were steaming water holes, but he had never encountered them. He bent down and put his hands in the water. It felt good to have warm water on his hands. He and his warriors had always washed the blood from their battles in the cold ocean water. His wife, Lagertha, was a shield-maiden and often fought beside Ragnar and did the same. The cold seawater awakened their senses and reminded the warriors of the many deaths of their enemies. Still, the warm water comforted his worried mind, and he was glad they would be resting beside it for the night.

Ragnar checked again to make certain that the stone was still next to his heart. He calculated that he could summon Ahmad sometime in the afternoon the next day. That will have been approximately an entire day since he placed it over his heart.

Ragnar knew that after Ahmad returned on the gryffon, the strange allies would need all of their strength and courage in order to be victorious. For now, he knew he must simply focus on his duty and everything would be revealed to him in due time. He let his eyes close for a while, thankful that he would have a short reprieve from his worries. Ragnar knew the gods were aiding them on their fateful journey.

8

Dragonfly Vision

by
H. M. Schuldt

In the morning they took off their clothes and bathed in the steaming water hole, which was deep enough to swim in. Ragnar took a flying leap into the air, tucked his knees up to his chest, and made a big splash. Karlo thought he looked like a big ball, and he laughed. The summoning stone lay on Ragnar's wet hairy chest. Steam swirled above the tranquil water. Ragnar missed his home, and so he stayed in the longest. An early sunshine came streaming through a crack and landed on Ragnar's skin. He noticed piercing rays of sunlight that seemed a little more reddish orange than normal.

***

Steaming water holes were quite common back in the Dwarf Mine of Davlin. The two dvergar set out to dry off away from the steamy cavern air. They were pleased to find an opening and make sense of their location. Karlo and Kerr sat on a shady rock eating chewy dried out meat and honey cake.

Soon Karlo instructed Kerr to gather a bag of rosy periwinkle down at a green grassy slope before high sun.

"Try to fill up the whole bag. We can use the extra," Karlo insisted.

"And we only need the petals?" Kerr asked.

"Yes. We will mix it with water from the mountain spring. Then we can sip on a tonic," Karlo confirmed.

Kerr marched alone through the stony spot and down toward the shady field of wild flowers to fetch a bag of petals.

Karlo had plenty to do while he waited for Kerr's return. He found a big flat shady area where he could make three liquids. Scorpion venom came in handy when there was time to use it. One would stay mild enough to relieve pain. The second would be able to knock anyone out. And the third would be deadly and good for arrow tips. He carefully labeled each one and placed three liquids in three separate waterproof pouches.

***

Sitting in the steaming water hole, Ragnar had plenty to think about, and he made sure the summoning stone remained in position to fulfill the one-full-day requirement. He did not worry about how to place the stone on his forehead or what was happening to Ahmad. Deep inside he knew that Ahmad would come back. And Ahmad's return was all Ragnar needed to be one step closer to getting out of the strange land and finding his way back to his wonderful mountain home in the North.

The furry man left the cozy water hole and dried off outside lying in the direct sun. He thought about the soul gem and the power it carried. He thought about his helmet, and wondered if he would ever see it again. He closed his eyes and imagined the three colors on the necklace. Sapphire. Emerald. Ruby. Big stones called out beauty and strength. Yet only one of them was made with a special power—so special that a lich will hunt for it. He thought about the danger that the maker of the necklace could be in. Something about the necklace pulled at him. He couldn't take it for himself. It wouldn't be safe for his wife either.

King Andren of the Dwarf Mine of Davlin knew the danger it held, and he was smart enough to get rid of the cursed piece of jewelry. Queen Valona had gone mad in her obsession to pursue it. She did not know how to handle the power it carried.

Cursed necklace must be evil, thought Ragnar. He sat peacefully in the warm sun alone with his eyes shut feeling hopeful that the Queen's ten warriors must be far away.

Dozing off in the morning sun, he saw a vision. An enormous dragonfly came buzzing directly at him. Ragnar had never seen an insect so big or imagined anything of the kind. It came closer carrying something in his two front legs. When its wings brought it gliding to the ground, Ragnar was so close that he could see his own reflection in the huge silvery eyes.

Ragnar wanted it to speak, but it did not say anything. The dragonfly did not stay long. It held a silvery item with three stones. Then it carried the item away and flew to a tree. It reached up to a branch and fastened the item. Ragnar tried to identify the object, wondering if it was a flute or a wind chime, but the object did not make any sound. A silvery stick dangled in the wind as he left it hanging in the tree. Just then a huge flying dragon came rushing from nowhere. It forced the dragonfly to go away. The scary looking creature took hold of the silvery stick. Was the dragon stealing it out of the tree?

The sight of the flying creature startled Ragnar. He woke up and quickly took his position as a fighter. It would be afternoon soon, and he had to be ready for Ahmad's return. At first he thought the vision could be a warning from his Father, a warning to watch out for dangerous flying creatures.

Ragnar learned from Karlo what to do with scorpion venom, but the furry man did not have any interest in trying to extract the poison himself unless he was forced to do so. He watched Karlo finish up the morning task of collecting three liquids for what Karlo referred to as attack and defense mechanisms. This type of fighting seemed rather odd and insignificant, but Karlo explained his duty to train other dwarves and to be ready to endure great hardships. "Suffering is a gift. In it is hidden mercy."

Ragnar decided to keep the vision to himself until he could figure out the meaning for sure. He knew Odin would not just warn him about dangerous flying creatures. He already heard about the dragon, Barrel the Terrible, so there must be more to figure out. He did not play a flute, and he wrongly guessed that maybe he should go look for one, which made him think about looking for Karlo's nephew.

"We should go look for Kerr," Ragnar said. His vision caused a greater sense for the three of them to stick together.

"I wonder what's taking him so long," Karlo said.

9

𝔄 𝔅eetle

by
Randall Lemon

"Let us hope he has not gotten into any mischief," groused Ragnar. "Odin knows there are so many evils chasing us that it is hard to decide which is most dangerous at any moment. Somewhere a frost giant hunts for me. The ten warriors of Queen Valona search for you and Kerr to take back the necklace for which she lusts in her madness. I am trapped in a land far from my own for some reason I cannot even now fully comprehend. And now, there is a lich—that evil undead sorcerer—who will never rest until he has the soul gem once again in the grasp of his skeletal hand."

At that very moment, they heard a rustling in the brush. Something was approaching them! Ragnar made ready to fight whatever it was. He gripped the haft of his trusty axe with both his hands. Many were the times when Ragnar had used this same axe to shatter the spine of the great Northern bears or to vivisect more human enemies. He would not succumb. He would destroy whatever danger threatened himself and the dvergar. If they could hold on, just a bit longer, he had every confidence that Ahmad would return. And with Ahmad's return, his chances to leave this place and return to his beloved tundra would increase dramatically.

Ragnar spread his legs assuming his warrior stance, one that allowed for the greatest possible power in his swing. Whatever it was in the brush was almost upon them. Ragnar began his stroke, just as Kerr came tumbling though the brush and straight at Ragnar. The veteran warrior was just able to check his swing, keeping it from decapitating young Kerr by bare seconds.

Not realizing the deadly threat he had just avoided, Kerr had a huge impish grin on his face. "Hail Ragnar, where is Karlo, I have found something that will surely bring a smile to his dour face." Ragnar could now see that the young dvergr had something clutched in one of his hands.

Karlo stepped forward with an angry expression on his face. "You young fool! Do you know how close you came to being killed? You came charging at us through the underbrush without a word of warning. Ragnar was ready to strike your impudent head from your body, not knowing if you were friend or foe! You must think about your approach much more carefully next time."

Kerr really looked at Ragnar for the first time and saw the warrior's grip on his axe. Realization struck the young dvergr like a rock. "I am most sorry. I went looking for medicinal herbs and didn't realize how far I had gotten away from the two of you. But look, Uncle, look what I have found. It is the best of all possible omens!"

Kerr carefully opened his fist showing his uncle, who did indeed gasp with astonishment. Ragnar looked over the top of the elder dvergr's head to see what Kerr was holding. The boy held a large bug in his hand, a beetle.

Ragnar was nonplussed. "What is so magnificent about this dung beetle you have in your grasp?"

Karlo turned to his large companion. "This is no ordinary beetle, It is one of the *sacred scarab beetles*. They are actually quite rare and seen as a great omen of good by our people. And the bigger the beetle, the greater good fortune it portends. Look at it size and color. This is a *regal scarab*. Something great is about to happen."

Ragnar stared at the beetle. Yes, it was quite large, almost as big as the palm in which Kerr held it. The beetle had a bright glowing color. *Is it more than just a bug? Is this a sacred beetle?* Ragnar thought. Suddenly he realized that this scarab was exactly the same size, color, and shape as the soul gem that rested against his chest. This was an odd coincidence.

It was then that the beetle began making a loud clicking noise. Its brightly colored carapace began to rise and fall with such rapidity that the three companions could not tear their eyes away from it. The creature's movements almost made its carapace seem to glow brighter and brighter. Light emanated from the scarab beetle. Was that heat Ragnar felt as well?

At that moment, Ragnar realized that the heat he felt was not coming from the beetle in Kerr's hand. Rather the gem that rested on his own chest was heating up. Looking down at the jewel, Ragnar could see it glowing with a corresponding brightness and color to that of the insect.

This was almost too much for Ragnar. Was there some magic afoot? Was it possible this bug was a wizard? The enormity of these unforeseen events made the wind seem to whistle around Ragnar's ears. What was happening?

Ragnar shook his mighty head as if to clear it. "Wait! There's a whistle. It's a rush of air from enormous wings—a flying creature—approaching us. Beware!!"

Ragnar spun around and looked to the sky hoping for the best but anticipating the worst.

10

Unexpected Visitors

by
Lynette White

Descending through the canopy was not one gryffon but *three*. Ragnar's mind flashed to the moment Ahmad was taken. As the majestic animals alighted, Ragnar searched the faces of the riders. None of them were Ahmad.

They consisted of two humans and a creature he could only explain as a human tree. What should have been hair was a tight mass of leaves. Its barely discernable face seemed to be formed out of a knot, but yet it had arms, hands, legs, and wore boots. As he looked closer, he realized the leaves covering the creature were the outline of a shirt and pants.

He was so mesmerized by the creature that he failed to realize the other riders were in motion. As a sign of respect, the gryffons stood before him in perfect military formation. It wasn't until the strange creature nimbly jumped from the gryffon's back that Ragnar understood the magnitude of the moment.

Each rider stood at full attention at the right side of their mount, their eyes locked on Ragnar. One of the riders made a sharp sound, and each rider drew their weapons. Ragnar instinctively tensed, and his body moved into warrior stance. He knew he would never win this fight, but if he was going to die, he was taking as many as he could with him.

He sucked in his breath as the riders repositioned their weapons, dropped to one knee, and lowered their heads in respect. His attention moved to the gryffons as one by one the majestic creatures also bowed their heads in respect.

"Blessed Odin," Ragnar whispered. "What is the meaning of this?"

A sudden movement in the big warrior's peripheral vision switched Ragnar's focus to Kerr. The young dvergr's jaw was hanging and his hand had dropped to his side. On the ground at Kerr's feet, the scarab was pacing, making a humming sound.

The creature held out its hand, but the beetle refused its invitation. The beetle began making the clicking sound again, and the tree creature responded. The entire conversation only lasted a few heartbeats. When they were finished, the creature ignored the beetle on the ground.

The tree creature straightened up to his full height. His voice was like the rustling of leaves. "The Gryffon Master has returned. And he summons his warriors."

Karlo nodded toward the tree creature and spoke sarcastically to Ragar. "Or he settled for something else."

Ragnar shot him an evil glare then looked down at the pacing scarab. Something was not right and the scarab was restless. Ragnar had come to trust the scarab, so he cautiously looked back at the riders. Ragnar's jaw dropped as he realized one of the riders was a woman. In her hand was a magnificent short sword. What captivated him was the way she carried herself. She wore comfortable clothes for riding, a perfectly tailored chain mail shirt, and her hair was tied back.

This woman was a strong warrior like his own beloved Lagertha. Not a single movement was wasted as she returned to her feet and cautiously started toward him. Her eyes darted between Ragnar and his axe.

Ragnar was so absorbed in the moment that he had not relaxed his position. Her steps were cautious as she tried to present a calm introduction. He lowered the axe and returned to a neutral stance. She came to a stop a safe distance from his axe and lowered her head.

"We have prepared for your return, Gryffon Master," she said.

Ragnar still could not wrap his head around this concept of being a Gryffon Master. "I am not..." he whispered.

She raised her head, and a smile tugged at the edges of her mouth. "Of course you are. Only the Gryffon Master can use the summoning stone to gather his warriors. We are the first, but soon the others will join us. There are nearly two hundred of us now."

I am expected to be a military leader? Ragnar thought. "But I did not summon you." He started to protest but stopped.

A sound of large wings once again echoed around them as seven more gryffons circled above the canopy, then settled to the ground one by one. Ragnar scanned them and frowned. Ahmad was not among them. The woman noted his disappointment.

"Do we not please you, My Lord?"

"No, that is not it." He quickly assured her. "It is just that I am expecting someone else."

She tilted her head quizzically. "Someone else?"

Karlo stepped forward and patted Ragnar on the arm. "He will be here."

"Who?" She pressed.

"Ahmad." Ragnar explained. "He was taken by a gryffon just after he picked up the crystal sword."

She suddenly sucked in her breath. "The Sword Master is here as well? Then our pleas to the gods were heard."

Ragnar blinked. "Excuse me?"

"Forgive me, My Lord. You must have so many questions and I will help you get the answers, but first allow me to introduce myself. I am Rachelle Trevlin from the house of Trevlin. My father sits on the throne in Afria."

Ragnar was not surprised she was royalty. "I am Ragnar Olafson. If you are a princess, why are you on a gryffon?"

"Lost princess by now," she corrected him. "Only my family knows of my calling as a Gryffon Rider. No doubt word has been spread across the nation that I am missing. A special group of men are searching for me, though no such rescue effort will ever happen."

Ragnar looked down at the ground. "I still do not understand why I am here, Rachelle." He looked back up at her, not even knowing if she was his enemy. "I am told it is my destiny to be here, but I cannot lead these people in a battle I know nothing about."

This time she allowed a smile to develop. "There is a small library that is carefully hidden to protect the secrets it holds. There you will find detailed records of the first heroes and the war they fought. I will take you there."

"I thank you, Rachelle, and I will accept your assistance. But I will not leave this spot until Ahmad arrives," Ragnar declared.

11

Sand Battle

by
Christian Warren Freed

Ahmad flew high above the world but took no wonder or joy from it. His face darkened with foreboding. Terrible thoughts skewed his perceptions, leaving him unaware of the majesty of the world. Gentle grasslands swept over rolling hills, broken only by rivers and streams. Small herds of animals Ahmad had never seen moved below. Birds gave him wide berth. Eagles and vultures gave the massive gryffon a second look before circling off to find easier prey.

Winds whipped into Ahmad's face and hair. His loose robes billowed forcing him to tighten his grip on the reins, lest he plummet to his death.

Death. He smirked. What terror does death hold for one who blissfully walks towards it? *I am no warrior but shall give my life to help this land and the Northman.*

His meeting with Faella left him deeply disturbed. She'd warned him of coming events, of a great confluence that would define the fates of two worlds. Ahmad's natural instinct was to deny, to refuse any part in it. He belonged in Jerusalem with the army, with his friends and countrymen, not as a soldier here. Ahmad had an important role to play. He had chronicled the military victories of the great Ṣalāḥ al-Dīn Yūsuf ibn Ayyūb from the battle of Hattin to the siege of Jerusalem. Very soon the Saracen armies would break the walls and retake the holy city. *Yet I will not be there to witness. Have mercy.*

His thoughts drifted back to his earlier conversation with Faella.

"You dream of your homeland but it is not yet time to return. This land is not finished with you."

"What use am I here? Everything is foreign. I do not belong," he defended.

Faella fixed him with a smile. "Ahmad, fate seldom asks if we want to partake in great events. This is one of those times. The real question is will you rise above all of your peers or fall into the dark cloud of obscurity?"

He paced the marble tiled floor. Warm sunlight flooded the chamber. Vines of lush green ivy draped down from the golden ceiling in sharp contrast to the panoramic views and white-gold marble. Ahmad searched deep inside his soul for answers. Answers that would not come.

"Clear your mind, and your heart will give you the answers."

Ahmad took a deep breath and did as she instructed. His mind suddenly opened with clarity he'd never experienced. He knew what he needed to do. Faella gave him a knowing grin.

"You must fly Rostok into the darkness to the west."

"But Ragnar is in the jungle."

"It is not yet time to find the Northman. There is a quest for you in the west."

Ahmad stiffened. "What will I find?"

"An endless sea of sand. Of your quest I cannot say, but that you shall know it the moment you see it."

Ahmad rode the gryffon into the darkness. Unimaginable cold stole the very warmth from his bones. He felt empty.

Despair wailed from a thousand throats. Phantom hands stretched forth to rip him from the saddle. Ahmad struggled to remain calm. Memories of his experience in the tower of gryffons held the dark images at bay for the moment. Still, he couldn't shake the feeling that something very bad loomed.

The ferocity of a sudden sound nearly ruptured Ahmad's eardrums. His very bones vibrated from the assault. Rostok jerked his head back and squawked defiantly. Looking down, Ahmad spied two massive creatures battling in the sand. Blood speckled the desert for a hundred meters around what looked like giant lizards. Coming from the desert, he had seen his share of lizards but never dreamed of a beast so large. Much less two of them.

One dragon was a dull gold. The other was black as the foulest nightmare. Both were huge, at least fifty meters from nose to tail. Their teeth were the size of a grown man. Razor sharp claws slashed and raked the other. As impressive as all of that was, Ahmad was drawn in by their jewel eyes. The gold dragon's were sapphire whereas the dark dragon's eyes were the foulest ruby.

Noxious fumes belched from the dark dragon's body, a poisonous miasma capable of killing the stoutest of creatures. The monsters attacked each other relentlessly. Ahmad watched in horror as the dark dragon barreled into the other, flipping the gold dragon, and exposing the vulnerable underside. It roared again, belching a cloud of flies and waste. The gold dragon struggled to roll upright, but was pounced on. Razor talons ripped into its soft flesh. Blood and scales fountained away. The gold dragon screamed.

Rostok must have read Ahmad's mind because the gryffon tucked back its wings and dove. Ahmad barely managed to draw the crystal sword. Wind slapped his face. The gryffon picked up speed, and down below the dark dragon reared up for the killing blow.

12

The Hut

by
Joyce Shaughnessy

The magic sword that Ahmad carried did its handiwork. Ahmad aimed straight for the belly of the dark dragon and swiftly slew him. As he lay in the last throes of death, Ahmad prayed, "Great is His Majesty, for giving me the gryffon and the power to slay the mighty beast."

The gold dragon continued to writhe in pain, but Rostok landed beside him, allowing Ahmad to dismount. Ahmad instinctively felt this creature possessed a *bountiful heart*, one worthy of saving. He laid the sword against the massive wounds on the dragon, and the injuries quickly disappeared, leaving him whole again.

Although the dragon couldn't speak, he stood in front of Ahmad and Rostok. Then he knelt in respect to give thanks. Ahmad bowed back, and the creature left. The Arab Bedouin was impressed with the dignity the gold dragon possessed and was grateful that the sword had given him the means by which he could save the gold dragon's life. He knew why the dark dragon needed to be killed. Ahmad realized the extent of his evil spirit when he saw him belching filth.

Ahmad knew that Ragnar needed him, but for some unknown reason, it was the one wish that couldn't be fulfilled by the crystal sword. His guess was that Ragnar would summon him when it was time for him to return. Until then he was forced to wait in this sea of sand.

***

Ragnar stood quietly with his axe in his hand. His impulse was to pull out the stone now burning and throbbing against his skin. He wondered why he simply didn't take it out now and summon Ahmad. Enough time had passed for him to do so, but something stopped him. Ragnar's instincts had made him the powerful warrior that he was, and he was inclined to obey them.

Rachelle repeated what she had said before, "I can show you where the library is hidden which protects the secrets of our heroes who fought in the Great War. Will you come with me?"

"I wonder, Rachelle, why you are so intent upon showing me this library of yours when I have told you that I am waiting for someone to return to me."

"You will need the secrets that the library holds."

Ragnar said much more forcefully, with his legs spread in a warrior's stance and his axe held in front of him, "Tell me the real reason why you want me to leave this place. Tell me why I should trust you and your gryffons. Why are there ten of you?"

"There is might in numbers."

"Evil may also exist in numbers."

Karlo gave a warning. "Ragnar, perhaps you should listen to her."

He turned to the dwarf and said, "And perhaps you should keep quiet."

As the man and two dwarves saw the beetle glowing, the ten gryffons and their masters suddenly turned into stone. They gasped at the sight, amazed at the transformation. The scarab beetle quickly scampered to Kerr, the dwarf who had found him, making loud clicking noises as he moved.

Ragnar said, "I thought that these ten warriors sent to me might be the ones whom Queen Valona sent to steal the necklace, but I had no idea how to defeat them by myself."

Karlo stood in amazement. "It must have been the beetle. It must dispense justice when malevolence is discovered. How extraordinary!"

"I must find somewhere secluded to concentrate on the summoning stone, away from any other dangers. We must find a place somewhere in this jungle."

The threesome searched through the dense thickets until they came upon a shelter in a dark part of the jungle. It was a strange little house that reminded Ragnar of the hut where Floki the shipbuilder lived. He felt that this was surely a good omen.

Inside the hut they found a strange troll, much like the one who had told them of the buried treasure and the summoning stone inside of it. He was ancient, like the forest where he lived. His hands were gnarled, and his back bent with age.

"Welcome, my friends. My name is Roland. I know who you are and why you have come to see me. I possess the power to see into the past and the future. Please sit."

Roland turned to Ragnar. "The stone you have pressed against your chest must be very warm, and I know that you are anxious to use it, but you must have some nourishment first." He served them warm beer and food from the forest. The food did not taste particularly good to Ragnar, but they hadn't eaten in several days.

While they were eating, a small monkey scampered out from a corner and landed on Ragnar's shoulder. He made chattering noises while consuming a large nut. The monkey had a white face and brown body. Ragnar had never seen a monkey before and was extremely nervous.

Roland laughed at his discomfort. "Don't worry. Capin is very friendly and seems to be quite taken with you. There are many monkeys in the jungle. They all sound different. You've probably heard them while walking among the tangled vines and trees."

"Yes, but I haven't seen any like this."

"Capin is helpful to an old man like me. He helps me by fetching fruit and nuts from the trees."

Ragnar stood. "I feel it is time that I use my stone as it was intended." He still felt a certain amount of distrust after the ten gryffons had almost fooled him.

He went into a dark corner of the hut and placed the stone on his forehead. Ragnar concentrated only on Ahmad, since those were the instructions given to him.

13

Summoning

by
H. M. Schuldt

As the Northman sat with his eyes closed in a dark corner, he held the comrade summoning stone against his forehead. Heat from the garnet traveled throughout his body, making him feel comfortable to carry out his duty. Even though Roland the Troll called it a quick return, ten minutes seemed like forever while holding the silicate to his own forehead. While sitting there he realized the call began twenty-four hours ago.

Ragnar earnestly desired for Ahmad's return and wanted him to bring the crystal sword. He kept his thoughts on the Sandman as he was instructed to do. He could feel the presence of the Sandman somewhere close by. The pull was getting stronger. It was then that he knew for certain that Ahmad was on his way, and his friend was traveling to help the furry man. Ragnar made sure to concentrate and to block out any distraction.

A knock came at Roland's door.

"Ahmad!" Karlo eagerly supposed, rushing toward the wooden door.

"It's only been five minutes," Roland observed. He took a deep breath sitting at the table. "Check the window."

Capin let out two low hoots.

"Who is it?" Kerr asked. He set down his periwinkle tonic.

"Someone I do not know." Karlo spoke with great disappointment. His eyes widened, and he prepared for an attack.

"Two hoots, and Capin says it's a messenger. Oh, what conflict!" Roland tightened a crumpled fist but kept himself from pounding it on the table. Immediately the troll saw it as a sign that the summoning might not be successful. He sent Karlo to open the door and instructed him to stay outside while he spoke to whoever it might be. "The summoning still might work if Ragnar can concentrate. Karlo, we need the visitor to go away as soon as possible."

"As you say," Karlo agreed.

Roland tried to hold his frustration because he should have kept someone outside to guard the door. He pushed back the guilt. There could be no more knocking, and Karlo would need to keep guard outside until the summoning was complete.

Kerr sat feeling overcome by the visitor's bad timing. He saw how the troll displayed regret and couldn't help but wonder if Ragnar was doing things the right way. Young Kerr made his decision to follow Karlo. He stood up and went to guard the front door outside along with Karlo. They had waited for one entire rotation of the planet to call for the Sandman, and he did not want to start over.

Karlo opened the door, and they saw a short little fellow who showed up at the wrong place at the wrong time. Karlo and Kerr stepped outside and shut the door. Karlo immediately informed the jolly little goblin about a special deed happening inside, "And we must speak quietly."

The messenger introduced himself as Guss the Courier. He announced that he needed to deliver both good news and bad news to Roland. "The bad news is that last night a jeweler named Jesper went missing. He was right in the middle of making a Rose Tessera for Queen Valona when he was captured. My report is that the forest creatures have seen a boneman, and they saw him take Jesper as a prisoner. It is believed that this boneman might force Jesper to make a magical stone. Unfortunately the undead skeletals want to command black dragons and keep them under control, that is, if they are lucky enough to capture one of those deathly beasts."

"And the good news?" Karlo asked.

"The good news," Guss said, "is that it takes at least thirty days to make a small magical stone, so I think we have plenty of time to intercept before the boneman runs off with a magical stone."

Karlo and Kerr stood speechless.

"Oh, and one more thing. Please take this and give it to Roland when you tell him the news." Guss the Courier handed a broken arrow to Karlo and agreed to wait outside for the troll's advice.

Kerr stayed outside guarding the door while Karlo went inside to quietly deliver the message to the troll. After hearing the news, Roland spoke softly so as to not disturb Ragnar's concentration.

"No visitors in thirty days, and then all of a sudden four strangers knock at my door in one day? My help is greatly needed. I will find someone to go rescue Jesper the Jeweler. Hmm. Most likely the lich will find a black dragon. The easiest way to defeat a black dragon is to cut off one of his toes. When his toe is cut off, he will forever lose his eyesight, and he will also lose his ability to guard the lich. But I will need to find out which toe must be cut off. Only a *champion axe* can cut off the toe of a black dragon." Roland responded to the threat out loud.

Karlo handed him the broken arrow. "A gift from Guss the Courier."

"Ah. Yes, for self-defense," Roland said.

"How so?" Karlo asked. "It is broken."

"The one who rescues Jesper will need fireproof armor. Black dragons are known for breathing the most deadly fire, blind or not blind. Karlo, my friend, these arrows are rare. This arrow is good for trading it in at the armor hut for one set of fireproof armor. And I will give this arrow to the one who is destined for this challenge."

Karlo refused to show any sign of lacking courage.

Ragnar slowly entered the room. He held out his hand. "The stone went cold."

"Odds are that the summoning did not work. For what reason, I do not know," Roland continued. "But fear not. It is possible to use the stone again as long as it does not turn dull or become foggy. The summoning instructions are simple, my furry friend. Now listen. Keep the red stone near your heart for one full day because the stone must be glowing bright and be ready to connect with the calling powers. Place the warm stone on the forehead. Concentrate on Ahmad and call upon his gryffon. Ask for their help. And do not be distracted by anything else during those ten minutes tomorrow. Which of these you did not do, I do not know."

"I didn't ask for help," Ragnar said. "And I didn't connect with the gryffon."

14

𝔥orgoth's 𝔖ecret

by
Randall Lemon

"Your rules are too difficult and remain unexplained. Where I come from everything is simpler. We live, we love, we fight and when a warrior dies, he is led by one of the beautiful Valkyrie to Valhalla the place of heroes. There he lives and loves and fights for all eternity until the great sword slips from its scabbard. Then Ragnarok and the end of days is upon us.

"In my world, trolls are evil and we slay them out of hand. Here they give me overcomplicated instructions on using magic stones to summon friends riding magical beasts. These friends have magical swords and will make it so I can destroy liches and other evil beings and save worlds like this one that does not even belong to me.

"When I roamed the tundra and frozen mountain ranges of my home, if I came upon a troll or frost giant or even a fire giant, I would take my battleaxe, Mästare, and vivisect the monster."

Roland stared at Ragnar sympathetically realizing that the furry man was justifiably frustrated by his failed attempt to summon Ahmad. "Perhaps you are too tired to try again immediately. Maybe a good rest would suit you well. As it turns out I have just received some disturbing news and must choose a course of action to follow. It is true we sometimes misunderstand each other, my friend from another world. We don't even speak the same language at all times. For instance when you were speaking just now, you used a word, *Mästare*. It sounded almost as if the axe you carry had a name, yet this word means nothing to me."

Ragnar hefted his beloved battleaxe in one hand. "*Mästare* is indeed the name of my weapon. It means *Champion* for I won it in a contest of warrior skills when I was quite young!" Ragnar said proudly.

Roland's attention was immediately galvanized.

"You are saying that this is your *Champion Axe*! This is amazing and most fortuitous. The gods have provided me with one answer even as we have been denied an immediate answer to our other problem, the summoning of your friend and his gryffon. It is you that will be our instrument in the destruction of the black dragon. Thus you can rescue Jesper from the clutches of the boneman. This will then deny the lich of attaining a new soul gem. You and your *Champion Axe* will make it so that the lich cannot work around our intent and will be forced to confront us!"

Once again poor Ragnar was completely mystified by what Roland was saying, but the troll seemed so happy and enthusiastic and the promise of slaying a dragon appealed to Ragnar. "Slow down my trollish friend, and tell me in detail what you mean. And if I can, know that I will aid you in saving this *Jesper* just as you are aiding me in summoning Ahmad."

Some time later the entire story had been explained to Ragnar's satisfaction, and he agreed to the adventure. "So, where do I go, and what must I do to slay the black wyrm?"

"There is a certain dvergr smith who was exiled from the kingdom of Queen Valona many years ago. He now lives not too far from this very spot. The glen where he has his smithy is magically hidden, guarded by objects that make his dwelling invisible to those who have not been gifted with the ability to see it by the smith himself. This dvergr is called Horgoth Anvilstriker. He is a craftsman of unsurpassable ability. I can direct Kerr and Karlo to the general area in which he lives, but you will not find him without this."

With that, Roland began rummaging through a trunk at the foot of his bed. Finally he pulled out a small candle and a single match. "When the two dvergar lead you to the glen, step into the area and light the candle. Only by its light will you be allowed to see the smithy and its master, Horgoth Anvilstriker. When Horgoth sees this candle, he will know that I have sent you to him. When you approach him, hold out this broken arrow to him and tell him I have sent you to obtain a set of fireproof armor."

Ragnar looked at the troll somewhat skeptically. "And he will make this enchanted armor for me in exchange for this broken arrow? And because I can see him because of a magic candle? This place grows stranger with every passing minute."

It was Roland's turn to roll his eyes, "No, you muscular midget! He will make it because he is my friend. He will make it because despite what you see with your eyes, this broken arrow is a talisman of great power. But most of all, he will make it because it is his destiny to do so. And if you want his very best efforts as a magical smith in creating this armor that may save your life, I suggest you tell him how defeating the dragon will help you defeat the lich which will then act to free Queen Valona's mind from the madness which has seized her. You see, Horgoth is the Queen's brother, and he was exiled when he spoke against her mad actions. No doubt he would like nothing better than to see his sister cured, so he can return to his beloved home once more."

So Karlo, Kerr, and Ragnar set off on yet another journey. As Roland had said, the two dvergar brought Ragnar to the edge of a glen, but the glen appeared empty. Doubting his own sanity, Ragnar stepped from the forest and into the glen. He took out a single match, struck it, and lit the candle. Immediately, the glen was transformed, and a large hut with an enormous smokestack stood in its middle. A muscular dvergr exited the hut and approached the trio. He stopped some paces from them and stared at the candle.

"I see you have the candle I made for my old friend, Roland. If my eyes are not failing me, it seems I recognize the two of you from my former home, Karlo and his young nephew, Kerr. Is it not? Follow me into my humble hut, and you can tell me why you have journeyed here."

When Ragnar entered Horgoth's hut, he was astonished to see no signs of a smithy's tools of the trade. There was no forge, no anvil, no smith's hammer, no ingots of metal, absolutely nothing with which to make armor, or anything else other than dinner. Nonetheless, he handed the broken arrow to the smith who eagerly accepted it and tucked it away.

There was a large fireplace, and above its mantle was hung a rusty notched sword. Ragnar stared at the sword intently. It was nothing but a Hobgoblin's spiked sword. It looked to be of poor quality and would be useless as a weapon in its current condition. He hoped this was not an example of the smith's skills. He wondered how far they would have to travel to arrive at his foundry.

They sat and Ragnar explained the entire story to Horgoth. When he talked of curing the madness of Queen Valona, he noticed a fire entering the eye of the dvergr.

Horgoth jumped to his feet. "We must begin immediately."

Ragnar stood more slowly, "Where will we have to travel to find your smithy?"

The smith gave a sly smile and turned to Ragnar. "You are standing in the middle of my foundry, you dunderhead. Give me that candle."

Shaking his head Ragnar handed the enchanted candle to Horgoth Anvilstriker. Horgoth set the candle down into the middle of his fireplace and, from his pocket, pulled a match. This match looked quite different from the one Ragnar had used earlier. It was longer and broader. It almost looked as if it were made of metal. Horgoth struck it against one of the bricks of his floor. A multicolored light shed forth, temporarily blinding the trio. When Horgoth touched it to the wick of the candle, the fireplace transformed into a huge forge already burning with a flame that was white-hot. Tables and chairs in the former hut turned into bellows and tongs. Piles of bright gray metal ingots appeared where once dishes had stood.

Dangling on a chain above the forge was the spiked hobgoblin sword. Horgoth immediately took some of the metal ingots and placed them into the forge. They glowed first red then white. The smith reached up and grabbed the hobgoblin sword and as his hand touched it, it transformed into a massive silver-colored smith's hammer.

He turned to the two other dvergar. "Man the bellows and put your backs into it!"

Then he turned to Ragnar, "Now my warrior friend, I will make you a set of Adamantine Chain Mail Armor, the likes of which has never been seen before. That dragon will not scorch you even a little. And in exchange, you will give me back my sister's sanity!"

Beads of sweat popped out on the brows of all four, as the smith began heating and turning and hammering and heating again. Ingots quickly began to transform into links of chain mail armor. And all the while he worked, Horgoth the smith sang of a black dragon's death!

15

Chain Mail

by
Lynette White

Ahmad plopped down and welcomed the comfort of the sand. This he understood—how it moved, how it was kind if it you knew how to befriend it, and yet how cruel and heartless it was if you failed to pay it homage.

He tried to clear his head but the close proximity of two parallel forces made it impossible. Evil still rolled off the dragon's foul body while the sword thrummed slightly in defiance.

Ahmad was admittedly a religious man, but all of his teaching and all of his faith did not prepare him for this place. He had never felt so lost in his entire life but yet so focused. He still did not fully understand his role in what was happening, but one thing he was certain of—his fate was linked to Ragnar.

His focus switched to the big warrior. Ahmad may have been snatched away soon after they met, but there was a deep bond between them—an old bond.

Ahmad focused on the dead wyrm and the claws in particular. Each claw was nearly as long as his forearm. The mere thought of what devastation those claws were capable of made him tremble.

He pushed himself to his feet and walked over to the closest foot, the left foot, as he remembered Ragnar's necklace of bones. He drew the sword and it flared to life in anticipation. With little effort, he severed two claws—one for himself and one for Ragnar.

Rostok looked at him and shook his head, making Ahmad doubt his action.

"Am I not to do this, Rostok? I just wanted something to take home to remind us of this place."

He held up one of the claws. "This is one thing Ragnar will cherish, and it might even bring him great power." He explained and dropped his hand to his side.

"For me, it will prove I have not lost my mind, and that I really was in this strange place." He added with a shrug.

Rostok suddenly tensed and moved closer to Ahmad, a deep warning growl rumbled in his throat. Ahmad looked around for the threat Rostok sensed but saw nothing. However, few heartbeats passed before he felt it—an evil matching that of the slain dragon.

Once again Ahmad felt the weight of despair and foreboding on his very being. Rostok was prepared to fight the unseen force and was so tense that Ahmad was afraid he would attack prematurely. His attention moved to the sword as it began to glow brighter than before. It, too, was ready to face this new foe. Ahmad climbed into the saddle without thinking, and Rostok sprung into flight so quickly Ahmad was nearly unseated.

They were barely a safe distance away before a black robed figure rushed toward the fallen wyrm. An ear piercing, blood-chilling scream came from the robed figure. Ahmad cringed, but Rostok screamed back.

The figured looked up, and Ahmad's blood froze as the same ruby red colored eyes glared up at him. A bony hand pointed at them. "You will pay for this with your soul, Sword Master!" The creature vowed.

***

Ragnar fidgeted with the armor. It did not sit right, was heavier than he was used to, and felt like it restricted his movement. Despite those issues, Ragnar had to admit it was the finest set of chain mail armor he had ever laid hands on.

Horgoth scratched his beard thoughtfully as he watched Ragnar. He snapped his fingers and wandered over to a large wardrobe in the corner. He yanked the doors open and began to mutter in a strange language. A flash of light could be seen in two of the drawers. Once again he began to speak in that strange language. Horgoth opened the top drawer, pulled something out, and tossed it at Ragnar's feet. He moved to the next drawer down, retrieving a second item.

He closed the wardrobe and spun around to present Ragnar with a new set of leathers. Ragnar eyed them, and then he looked suspiciously at Horgoth.

"These will solve your problem, lad. Those clothes you have on are too bulky for such a fine set of armor." Horgoth announced.

"But I like my clothes." Ragnar started to protest.

Horgoth snickered. "Oh, yes, your clothes are perfect if you want to look like one of Roland's monkeys. But suit yourself. You can be comfortable and respectable in these or continue to fight with your stupid pride."

Ragnar knew Horgoth was right and reluctantly took the new leathers from him. "And what if these do not fit?"

Horgoth just laughed. "They will fit."

Ragnar moved off to a corner and stripped off his old clothes. He hesitated. At home, before a man donned new battle gear, he cleansed himself. It represented washing the past away and starting new. Needless to say, it was not something one did lightly.

He could not help but see this as one more step taking him farther away from home, but he would not give up that easily. As an act of blatant defiance, he folded his old clothes and put them in his pack.

Now the armor settled into place and did not feel so binding. Ragnar was forced to admit the new leathers were softer and much more comfortable than his native wear.

"We must be returning to Roland's." Karlo stated. "Ragnar must rest so he can focus on the summoning tomorrow."

They said their goodbyes and started out of the glen. When they reached the edge, Ragnar turned back, but the glen was again empty. He touched his new armor to remind himself it was real. "Blessed Odin, if I do not lose my sanity before the end of this, I will be surprised." He remarked and shook his head.

Karlo heard him and chuckled. "I have a feeling that is going to be the least of your concerns."

They were almost to Roland's when the air around them turned cold, and the sound of splintering trees echoed from the left.

"Watch out, lads! The frost giant has finally caught up!" Ragnar shouted and pulled out his axe in preparation for the next battle.

He touched his new armor. "I hope this is as good against cold as it is suppose to be with fire." He quietly remarked and prepared himself for battle.

16

The Prophecy

by

Christian Warren Freed

"What evil is this?" Ahmad whispered.

As fell powers radiated on the air, Ahmad swooned. Darkness cringed around the edges of his vision. Rostok lowered his head, arching out his massive wings, and hissed a baleful growl. The figure in black laughed.

"You should tame your pet," he hissed.

Ahmad slowly drew his sword. A strange combination of light and dark radiated off of the crystal. "Be gone from here, Djinn. I have no quarrel with you."

Another laugh—this time mocking—disturbed the air. Vibrations buzzed in Ahmad's ears. Blue fire erupted from the palm of the Djinn's hand. "Do not think, mortal, to command one of the *chosen*. Your soul will suffer for your crime."

"What crime? I slew a fell beast and saved a good one. My soul is not yours to barter with. Now be gone or meet my blade."

The Djinn mocked him openly. "You cannot kill me, boy. I am eternal."

"We shall see," Ahmad snapped and leaped toward the Djinn.

His enemy barely moved. Sand and earth erupted, knocking Ahmad backwards. Rostok screeched and took to the air. The Djinn lashed out. Dark bolts of power went from his fingertips to the gryffon's chest. Feathers and fur singed. Rostok plummeted to the sand. Ahmad watched his companion crash into the ground. Pain lanced his chest when he tried to move. His body ached. Smoke sizzled off of his cape and armor. The Djinn spread his arms. Ahmad could feel the evil—the pure hatred—radiating from the ancient creature.

Struggling, Ahmad rose first to his knees and then, shakily, managed to stand. As if showing a modicum of respect, the Djinn waited until Ahmad brought the crystal sword in front of him before unleashing a devastating blast of power. The sword caught the blow, though Ahmad was still driven back several feet. Teeth grit and muscles straining, he pushed back against the evil. It was a losing effort. Ahmad knew now how he lacked the strength to defeat one of the Djinn.

He never saw the arrow zip past his head and plunge into the Djinn's dark heart. Caught off guard, the Djinn failed to prevent the second or the third from striking. He stopped his assault on Ahmad and—in a great show of power—collapsed in on himself. Blue and green waves of energy coalesced over the battlefield and then nothing. It was done.

Ahmad passed out and knew darkness. When he awoke both he and Rostok were in a crudely built structure. Pinpricks of sunlight stabbed down through the reed laced roof. He tried to rise but the pain forced him back down.

"You are in no position to move yet," a child-like voice said from behind him.

"Where am I?" Ahmad looked around hoping to find the source of the voice.

A squat green-skinned figure ambled into his line of sight. Large batwing ears protruded from the sides of his head. His eyes were small and pecking. His face was long and pinched. Patches of grey-black hair spotted his head and arms. Ahmad winced at the nauseating smell wafting off the creature.

"You are here safe. What in the name of nine scepters were you doing out here alone? Only a fool would risk his life so."

Ahmad managed to prop himself up on an elbow. "I am not here by choice. Many thanks to you for saving my companion and me."

The green creature eyed him suspiciously. "Your companion has eaten too many of my comrades to be welcome under normal conditions, but the dark ones are a greater evil. I am Hygliak."

"Ahmad Ibn Fazzat. What manner of creature are you, Hygliak?"

"I'm a goblin, a scout for the king's army. And you, Ahmad Ibn Fazzat, shouldn't be here."

Ahmad shook his head. *Goblin?* He'd never heard of the like. "What king? What army?"

Hygliak paused setting down the cup of vile brown liquid he was about to give Ahmad. "You're truly not from here, are you?"

"No. I was taken from my homeland and dropped off in a dark jungle with another—a Northman. My life has been an unending struggle since." He looked around the building, noticing for the first time the vast extent of weapons filling the walls and the lone wooden table on the far side. "This is an arms room?"

"Yes, one of many. I told you I am part of the king's army." Hygliak poured the liquid into a small bowl. "Here, drink this. It will help you recover your strength. We are marching to war against the lich king. It is my job to clear the avenues of approach and guide our army as best I may."

"Many strange things have befallen me. That is how I came into the company of a gryffon and carry the crystal sword." Ahmad reached for his weapon only to discover it wasn't in its sheath.

Hygliak laid a comforting hand on his shoulder. "Relax, friend. Your sword is right here. Take this dragon scale shield. It seems they were both made for you. Perhaps your coming to our land was fortuitous in more ways than one."

"What do you mean?"

"There is a prophecy that two men shall come to save us from the terrible curse afflicting our kingdom. One will be of pale skin and a fierce warrior. The other shall have dark skin and be a great thinker. Together they will end the curse of the lich king and return peace to our lands."

Ahmad struggled to comprehend what he'd just been told.

I'm no hero, no great warrior, no thinker. I'm just a man.

He felt exhausted. Too much had happened—leaving him at sanity's brink.

Seeing this Hygliak said, "Rest now. We should be safe here for the remainder of the night. In the morning we will continue north. I must take you to meet the king."

17

Trouble at Yggdrasil

by
Joyce Shaughnessy

Ragnar placed his legs apart in a fighting stance as the chilling cold settled on the three travelers. Kerr and Karlo had never seen nor fought a frost giant and were understandably apprehensive. Ragnar had once been forced to slay a frost giant in battle, but never in this strange land, and he wondered if the creature would be fiercer. The earth shook, and the giant roared as the bone chilling cold quickly developed on the branches of the trees in the forest making them visibly icy.

Suddenly the trees parted. *Crack!* Breaking through icy branches, the giant came forth.

"Holy Odin!" Ragnar exclaimed. "It is the largest one I have ever seen. It is the mighty Skyrim brought to life again! Father, help me save my mortal soul and these dvergers with whom I am destined to travel."

The giant suddenly paused in the path, and Karlo ventured to Ragnar's side. "Give me an arrow, Ragnar. I can dip it in a poisonous liquid made with scorpion venom. Quick!"

Ragnar rapidly plunged his arrow into the poisonous liquid. Karlo aimed it and fired into the shoulder of the giant. Ragnar's Champion Axe was next as Ragnar thrust it into the right side of the giant. Karlo and Kerr audibly drew in their breath as the frost giant laid his mighty right paw on Ragnar's shoulder and squeezed, but his strength seemed to leave him in the same motion. The giant released the Northman and retreated into the trees taking the ice and frigid wind with him. His shriek of dismay and pain could be heard throughout the forest. Ragnar collapsed on the ground.

The two dvergers quickly ran to his side. Karlo reaching for some healing medicine when Ragnar weakly said, "I am all right, just sapped and bruised. You saved us from certain death." He closed his eyes and slept.

Afternoon was well upon them by the time Ragnar rose from the ground and found the two dvergers asleep. He shook them awake and said, "We must go. I must find shelter where I can concentrate on the Summoning Stone. I can feel in my bones that the Sandman and his gryffon are in trouble. Let's leave this place."

The three men headed down the trail. Soon they arrived at a place even more isolated where the vines intertwined in a similar but heavier pattern. There was almost no sun coming through the thick jungle. Ragnar announced that this might be a place where he could concentrate and bring Ahmad back.

And it was then that he saw it—an ash tree so tall and so wide that it disappeared into the heavens dwarfing all of the other trees in the jungle. Ragnar stood in awe of it. He exclaimed, "It is the blessed Yggdrasil!"

A large squirrel suddenly appeared. Ratatoskr's body was five feet long, with a tail half as long and a large horn between his ears. He could be heard murmuring under his breath, "A lich is upon you. He will transport one of you to the world of the wyrm, Nodhogrr, who dwells below the earth and gnaws on the roots of the blessed tree." He quickly scampered up the large ash out of sight.

Karlo grasped onto the trinket around his neck to confirm that he was still under safe protection for one more cycle of the sun, but when Kerr went to reach for his trinket, he found that it was gone.

"Norseman, is it this easy for me to sneak up on you and your two dwarven companions? If so, your life will be short indeed." A malevolent voice spoke from behind while Kerr looked in haste for his trinket to see if it was in his shirt. Karlo spun around and saw the ancient lich's flickering red eyes, his bones clothed almost in darkness. The lich pointed his long skeletal arm. "The young dwarf is yours in exchange for the soul gem."

A bright blue flame erupted from his fingers. Immediately, Kerr and the lich disappeared!

Complete darkness overwhelmed Karlo and Ragnar. With it came the question of victory or defeat. They knew that the deceitful lich could not be trusted to keep his bargain. Perhaps Kerr's soul had already been sucked from the dwarf's young body turning him into one of the mindless undead destined to serve the lich in the world of Nodhoggr for eternity. The two travelers must draw on their intelligence in order to save their comrade, Kerr.

It would also take a miracle to escape the confines of the jungle that entrapped them. Ragnar's mere strength of body had been their salvation before, but now with his strength sapped by the frost giant, he doubted his ability to save them. Nor would his strength bring the Sandman to them. Sadness gripped him, but Karlo refused to show any sign of despair.

***

Ahmad was filled with compassion for the badly wounded Rostok who lay beside him, but he thought about the vitality potion given to him by Faella. Should he give it to Rostok? The answer was obvious. Without the gryffon, he would never be able to return to Ragnar. It was the only way to escape this mad world of dragons and liches. He was convinced that Rostok was part of his destiny.

Just as he was about to pour the crucial liquid into the unconscious gryffon's mouth, Rostok's large head turned toward him. Ahmad poured some of the powerful liquid into Rostok's mouth. Almost immediately, Rostock rose and trembled on his powerful legs, but a few minutes later, he was steady. He gazed at Ahmad with love and warmth in his big brown eyes.

Ahmad quickly returned the pouch to his belt and stood beside the powerful gryffon—proud to be his friend and comrade. They were ready to join the goblin, Hygliak, on a journey north to meet his king.

18

City in the Sand

by
H. M. Schuldt

Ahmad agreed to travel to the peaceful sand city of Sanyogita where Rostok could rest. Camels would take them to a king in the desert. Hygliak knew that inside the city it was normally safe because the Sanyogitans believed in trade and in a peaceful loving life. Sand liches had been causing turmoil near the ancient tombs outside of the city, so they had to be ready for anything. Rostok sailed over the dunes and landed at the edge of the sand city. They found a small oasis filled with large palms and cool shade for Rostok to rest for a while. The gryffon settled in a private spot near a small spring protected by rocks and cushioned by soft grassy plants.

Hygliak lead his tall friend through rolling white dunes where bunches of acacias stood like crooked skeletons. The scout goblin was dressed in faded blue robes lined in dark decorative stitching covering his green arms and legs. His head and face was covered in a keffiyeh of shimmering indigo protecting against any sand storm, but his two large batwing ears pierced through. Two camels stood prepared stately and calm with fluffy hides as pale as the sand beneath their hoofs.

Two single humps were outfitted with high-back saddles of balsam-light wood striped with blue and gold. They paid for the traveling service, mounted the saddles, and set off to meet the Sand King of Sanyogita.

In the distance they saw the Temple of Life behind thick magnificent palms. As they drew near Ahmad noticed a long pier extending out into the hot dry sand. A tall wooden platform allowed them to dismount with ease. They tied their camels to a pole and walked down the long wooden boardwalk. The sun felt warm as it burned through the dust clouds. Hygliak spoke to a Sanyogitan with a quaint dialect. His delicate inflections reminded Ahmad of twittering birds drifting in a dreamy sky.

Outside the temple in the courtyard, men lounged puffing on handmade cigarettes, tan shemaghs pulled up to their eyes. Twelve teenage girls giggled and chatted. Their long hair was woven into braids affixed with silvery bangles. Several older women walked outside, and one carried a goatskin drum. A melodious verse began which sounded familiar to Ahmad. Two teenage boys leaped from a datepalm and into the center extending brown arms to the side and kicking feet into a war dance.

"You're in luck, my friend," a Sanyogitan spoke next to Ahmad. "Today is a special day for the king."

"What is this drama?" Ahmad asked.

"The king has people praying inside his temple everyday, but today we honor the treasure of youth, and tonight we open beer jugs."

Another woman shook a tambourine, and the girls launched into spitfire clapping. Complementary rhythms brought glory to banshee cries as the men relaxed and lowered their shemaghs. The girls lined up swaying together as they chanted with strength and beauty. They moved their hands in ornate twists as silver bracelets jingled on their wrists and silver rings covered their fingers. They shined forth a joy for the passion of dance and song celebrating life and power in the deadly desert. The air was intoxicating with the narcotic fragrance of blue lotus, and Ahmad forgot about Hygliak's stench. He even forgot about Ragnar.

Everyone turned when they heard a loud shout approaching, "Yiiiip! Yiiip!" Ahmad saw two teenage boys, one bald and the other one almost completely shaved but with a long braid on the side. They charged in on two camels galloping across the sand. The long-legged camels gracefully bounced across the soft white sand. The camel races had begun. This performance was not to defeat an opponent but to display a great skill for the Sand King of Sanyogita who appeared on a second level stone balcony.

Ahamad stood in the small crowd and felt the unity. He knew the passionate tongue in which they chanted.

There is one in the spirit! Yes, there's one! Yes, there's one!
They will know we are mighty! We have won! We have won!
Love will lead us! Love will lead us! Lead us on! Lead us on!

Ahmad missed his home in the sand. He stood there watching camels run majestically back and forth. Two young teenage warriors rode past raising an arm yelling, "Peace to all!" and "For the love of life!" It made him think about a world in which all is pleasant—a true paradise on earth. He looked upon the youth and knew it would be most happy for newlyweds to marry because of their love for one another.

There must be a circle of protection around this temple in the desert, thought Ahmad. He felt privileged to see it.

Ahmad forgot all about grave robbers and liches. He forgot all about Ragnar, and he forgot to be on guard. This joyous celebration overwhelmed all his senses to the point of having no fear of anything. He wanted this protection to last for all eternity.

Suddenly one of the black dragon claws pressed against his leg, and the worst possible dread came over him. It made him reach into his pocket and take a drink of Faella's vitality potion.

19

Sand Skimmer

by
Randall Lemon

The pressure on his leg from the black dragon's claw continued to increase until Ahmad felt as if it were trying to bore its way into the flesh of his legs. He began to tear at his clothing and claw madly at the point where the claw was making contact with his tender flesh. His efforts, however, were stymied because he couldn't get at it to relieve the pain. Now he spun, wildly grabbing and jumping, trying to relieve the pain. Why did no one help him? Could they not plainly see his agony?

He looked around at the woman with her drum, the twelve young dancing girls with their bangly bracelets, the two young men, and even his companion the goblin, Hygliak. Ahmad was surprised to see that they froze—watching him. Their faces were painted with broad smiles and joy touched the corners of their eyes.

As Ahmad continued to hop frantically about the sand near the pier before the Temple of Life, Hygliak finally shouted exuberantly, "My friend Ahmad, truly it is a wonder! You never told me that you were the very best and most skilled of Dervishes!"

Hygliak grabbed two of the curved desert blades from the sashes of the men who stood by smoking their cigarettes and then tossed them into the air toward Ahmad. Without any conscious effort, Ahmad caught both blades at the midpoint of a spinning leap into the air taking him over the head of one of the dancing girls. He knew not where this sudden ability came from, but he landed lightly again on the sand. He began to move the blades in a dizzying pattern—fast...faster...faster! The movement of the blades became a blur, and Ahmad behind the blades blurred as well.

Smoke began to rise from the rapidly vacillating form of Ahmad and disaster appeared imminent.

Just then another blur appeared out in the desert heading directly at the pier that jutted out from the Temple of Life. Was this some new horrible Djinn seeking revenge on the people of Sanyogita? Perhaps it was one of the gigantic sand slitherers or a fire elemental whose heat caused the shimmering effect that hid its true form?

Instead, at what seemed to be the last possible moment, the form turned and slowed and pulled directly up to the pier. It was beyond doubt the sleekest and most beautiful sand skimmer ever seen. This desert ship was covered with golden adornments and carved on its prow was an intricately created figurehead of a golden dragon. On the side of the ship in garish letters was painted its name, *Blessed of Bahamut*.

Ahmad continued to twirl just ten feet in front of the sand skimmer. Suddenly a voice rang out from the deck of the ship. It was a voice as clear as a clarion call, "Now my brothers release the breath of Bahamut on this bedeviled fellow."

From the mouth of the figurehead spewed a golden concoction that appeared to be made of equal parts of sand, water, and smoke to those who were fortunate enough to observe this miracle. The spray struck Ahmad with the force of a sandstorm, and yet not a single person near Ahmad was touched by it.

As the mixture hit Ahmad, he was thrown from his feet and down onto his back in the sand. He struck with such force that he bounced twice. But then as his now inert form came to rest, darkness rose from the thigh of Ahmad. It rose into the air and hung there for a moment. Then with a shriek of such unadulterated evil that all who heard it had their hair stand on end, it streaked into the sky and disappeared from sight.

A single man swung down on a rope from the ship above, landing on the sand next to Ahmad. The man had a pointed black beard and a thin black moustache. His full hair was gathered in a single braid that descended down his back all the way to his waist, and his eyes were the color of the desert sky.

Frightened though he was by recent events, Hygliak moved toward the helpless form of Ahmad preparing to defend him from this man whose ship had struck him down. The goblin tried to place himself between Ahmad and the newcomer. "Who are you and why have you struck down my friend?"

"As to who I am, little man, my name is Abdullah bin Khaleel ur Rahman. I am the Captain of the sand skimmer, the Blessed of Bahamut. I struck down your companion not to hurt him, but to heal him. Did you not see the evil spirit rise from him after he was bathed in the blessed breath of Bahamut? It is a good thing for you and all those gathered here that I arrived when I did. My crew and I were on our way to Sanyogita to resupply and to participate in your Festival of Life when our seer, Amineh Afshan had a vision of the evil that had descended upon you. She urged us to put on all sail and speed to your rescue."

At that moment, a moan escaped the lips of Ahmad and he began to stir. Hygliak knelt next to Ahmad's head. One of the dancing girls arrived with a skin of water that was placed to the parched lips of Ahmad. In fact, on closer inspection, the face and body of Ahmad was red and shriveled as if he had been wandering beneath the unforgiving desert sun for days.

Finally Ahmad appeared recovered enough to croak out some words, "Is the music evil? I listened to the music and suddenly my very essence was black with anger. When you tossed me the swords, Hygliak, I knew it was destined that I should kill all these false worshippers at this Festival of Life, especially the king of these evil idolaters. But why? I bear these people and their king no ill will. Somehow I was released from the musical trance that had captured my soul."

Now the ship's captain knelt next to Ahmad. Taking the tulwar from his sheath, he began to cut away at the clothes near Ahmad's thigh revealing a deep puncture wound. "The music itself was no more evil than any other music that is played at any one of the sand festivals celebrated by the people of this desert. The poison entered you through this wound and allowed your possession."

Now Abdullah inspected the claw itself. "This is not just a claw of any black dragon you have here my friend. Unless I am mistaken this claw comes from the talon of a dragon that was a consort of the evil dragon queen herself, Tiamat. Your spirit must be very strong, not strong enough to resist this evil, but strong enough not to be lost forever in its labyrinth of foul darkness. Had you whirled much longer you would have been owned entirely by the Master Dark Dervish. You would have become a Dark Dervish who serves Tiamat. You could have killed all these kind people and their king. Your soul could have been bound to Tiamat forever and her allies, the desert liches. Who knows what evil they would have required you to do.

"You might have been turned into an assassin and sent to destroy your own family or even your best friend. You would have even relished these dark acts—for they would bring pleasure to the evil queen of dragons. Luckily the evil contained in the claw has been expelled, and it cannot return. Although your flesh will be weak for some days to come, you will find your spirit so strong that it appears to be the essence of iron. You will be able to resist any possession except from the absolute strongest of sources. Even evil that great will find it no easy thing to turn you toward the darkness again."

20

The Third Human

by
Lynette White

Kerr instinctively curled up into a ball to make himself as invisible as possible and to protect himself from the darkness that threatened him. His entire body trembled uncontrollably, but it was impossible to tell if it was the bone chilling cold or soul crushing fear pulling at the very fabric of his being that caused it.

He had never experienced fear and hopelessness like this, but a part of him was still determined to fight. He was on the brink of giving into despair when his mind slowly began to acknowledge the sound of a steady clicking.

His terrified mind locked onto the sound, and his fear weakened. As he fought his way back, his body slowly unfolded. Finally he ventured to open his eyes. Kerr was in absolute darkness but found comfort in the clicking sound. As long as the sacred scarab was with him, Kerr knew he would somehow rise above this.

"Hello, my friend. I am glad to hear you are near. I am in a bad spot here."

The clicking sound grew louder and a faint light pierced the darkness. An audible gasp came from somewhere in the darkness.

"It cannot be." A faint voice spoke.

Kerr started at the sound of another voice, and someone moved toward him. "Who is there?"

The person stopped moving. "I am Jesper. Please tell me who you are and how you have a sacred scarab as a companion?"

Kerr sat up. "Jesper? We received word you were taken. My companions and I were to search for you as soon as Ahmad returns. This sacred scarab has saved Ragnar, Karlo, and myself more than once."

Jesper moved closer, and Kerr gasped as his bruised and swollen face came into the scarab's faint light. The scarab's clicking became more insistent and Jesper retreated back into the darkness, embarrassed by the mutilation he had suffered at the hands of his captors. Jesper whimpered in fear as the scarab moved up his arm and settled on his head.

"Do not be afraid, Jesper, I am certain he is trying to help you." Kerr advised him.

A golden light slowly bathed Jesper's entire head and the captive dvergr quietly sobbed as his bruised and broken face healed.

"Thank you," Jesper whispered. The light slowly faded to a faint glow and the scarab returned to Kerr's side. "They have no mercy for those who do not bend to their will."

"Have they forced you to start the stone?"

Jesper's face moved back into the light. "How do you know about that?"

"A messenger told us when he brought us a broken arrow, so Ragnar could get his armor. So have you?"

Jasper's head dropped. "Not yet. I keep telling them I need the perfect stone. I have been hoping I could stall long enough to find a way to escape." He admitted and looked back at Kerr. "Who is this Ragnar you speak of? That is an odd name."

"Ragnar is a great warrior from another land, and so is Ahmad—though I have never met him. They are the men prophesied to free our land from this evil. Ragnar is the Gryffon Master, and he has the summoning stone. Ahmad has the Crystal Sword but, for reasons we do not understand, a great gryffon has taken away Ahmad. And now Ragnar is trying to summon him back."

Kerr reached into the darkness and found Jasper's arm. "We have to stall the Lich King and somehow get word to Ragnar."

***

Ragnar and Karlo stared at the spot where Kerr had been standing. Then they looked at each other. Karlo shook his head ever so slightly and turned his attention to the lich.

"If you think I will fall for your lies, you do not know the mind of a dvergr," Karlo said. "Kerr would surrender his life before he would break a sacred vow and disgrace his tribe."

"We shall see." The lich hissed and drew the darkness back to himself. A heartbeat later he was gone.

Karlo released his breath. "At least we stalled him."

Ragnar's axe suddenly felt heavy, and he lowered his arm. "But for how long, Karlo? We need Ahmad. I have got to find some place to think."

Karlo patted him on the arm. "I know, my friend. We best get moving."

They did not go far before the sound of something moaning brought them to a stop. Ragnar drew his axe and cautiously moved toward the sound.

He nearly missed the man—human like himself—dressed in green and sitting against a tree. His knees were drawn up and he clutched his stomach. His face was pale and sweat dripped from his chin.

Ragnar stopped in his tracks, and Karlo nearly crashed into him. He deftly sidestepped Ragnar and groaned as he looked at the man.

"He has the jungle sickness. Poor soul." He walked toward the man.

"Karlo, wait."

"He will die if I do not help him, Ragnar. I have herbs to save him." Karlo knelt down beside the human. Ragnar sighed and followed.

"I am Karlo. I can help you."

The human's head moved in the direction of the voice, but his eyes were still unfocused. "I ran out...need herbs..." the human muttered.

"Yes, yes, I know." Karlo slid his pack off his back. He rummaged through it until he found a leather belt with several small pouches and vials of liquid. He grabbed a vial of blue liquid, and coerced the human to swallow it. Then he opened one of the pouches and grabbed a pinch of the herb. He placed that under the human's tongue and returned the belt to his pack.

He stood up and slung the pack over his shoulder. "That might get him back on his feet in a couple of days. We need to get him out of this heat." He started to survey the area. A chimney nearby caught his eye. He pointed in the direction of what he assumed was the man's house.

"I am guessing he came from there. Can you carry him that far?"

Ragnar followed Karlo's finger and calculated the distance. He had carried his own wounded soldiers much farther. He looked back at the human.

"I can. But what about…"

"You can only get jungle sickness from the bite of a blue winged jungle fly." Karlo quickly assured him, addressing this fatal concern.

Ragnar's hand moved to his chest. "The summoning stone is warm again. I have to help Ahmad. He might be in trouble."

Karlo shrugged. "One place is probably as good as another. I am guessing this man is a solitary woodsman. If anyone else was around here, they would be looking for him."

21

𝔖tranger in a 𝔖trange 𝔏and

by

Christian Warren Freed

Ahmad stared up at Abdullah bin Khaleel. Soft winds kissed his weathered face reminding him of a simpler time. He closed his eyes and saw the great muster east of the Jordan River where ten thousand Saracen fighters gathered under the banners of the great Saladin. The road from Damascus to Jerusalem lay open to the invading army. Those days were all but a dream now. He was a stranger in a strange land—a wanderer lost in a world he didn't understand or wish to be in. Ahmad started to believe he might already be dead, and the purity of his soul was being tested. How else could he explain the wondrous and horrible sights he'd bore witness to?

"You have much going on behind your eyes, my friend," Abdullah said with a knowing look. "I offer you passage aboard my vessel. My eyes tell me you could use a long respite."

Ahmad sighed. "If only I could, but I am not alone here. There is another that I must hasten to."

"What better way to search than by my ship?" Abdullah didn't want to take no for an answer. "We can cover ground more quickly than on foot."

Ahmad smiled. "I agree, but I have my own vessel. His name is Rostok."

"Ah, the gryffon. It takes a special man to control such a beast." He rose. "Very well. May fortune favor you, Ahmad. There will come a time when we shall meet again."

"I look forward to it," Ahmad replied.

"Until the winds blow us in the same direction, goodbye."

Ahmad watched Abdullah stride away, a strange sense of accomplishment in his thoughts. He didn't know why, but following the same course was the proper thing to do. Perhaps it was the sword gently thrumming at his hip or the primal urgings of the winged beast he had healed. He couldn't say. After all, he was just a man. And man was faulty at best.

"It would have been nice to ride for a change," Hygliak said unexpectedly.

The Arab almost forgot about the goblin scout. They'd traveled far and had gotten along well enough on the road, but Hygliak needed to go back to his king and their campaign. Time fled from them both.

Ahmad nodded. "There are some things a man must do, friend Hygliak. Tell me, where does your king march to?"

"We go to fight the great evil in the darkness," Hygliak replied glibly. "You know of which I speak. You have already felt it, fought it. This war will determine the fate of our world."

Of course, Ahmad realized, all of the negativity he'd struggled against. All the hatred and underlying malevolence. It was all leading him towards the inevitable conclusion that the darkness was already at war with him. Ahmad grinned ruefully. He knew what he needed to do.

"Hygliak, I must find the man I arrived with. It is important."

The goblin shrugged. "We each have our purpose."

"I only pray there is light at the end."

Cocking his small head, Hygliak asked, "What troubles you?"

Ahmad took a deep breath. "I fear I may never return home. So much stands against me. How can anyone overcome such incredible odds?"

"You will or you will not," Hygliak replied.

"That is not encouraging." He couldn't help but think how easy it would be to give up, to turn around, and find another way home. He didn't know Ragnar and certainly didn't owe the Northman anything. In his own time and world, they would have been mortal enemies on different sides of theological enmity. Still their brief time together at the beginning of this nightmare left him with a vague sense of brotherhood. Ahmad had the feeling that Ragnar was in over his head, and the noose was closing.

"There is a difficult choice ahead of you. If it pleases you, our paths follow the same course. I would like to journey further with you," Hygliak offered.

Ahmad was flattered. He was a stranger in a strange land. Any form of friendship was appreciated though he had never felt so alone. Conflicted, Ahmad got to his feet. There was much yet ahead of him and none of it was certain. Rostok padded over to him and lowered his head. Hygliak placed his hands on his hips and waited.

Time slowed. The winds picked up gently tossing sand across his face. He was tired and wounded. He missed the familiar scent of salt on the sea and the endless miles of marching through the holy land.

Slowly and after much deliberation, Ahmad nodded. "Very well. Let us continue this strange journey and see what our destiny has in store for us."

22

Lizard Goblin

by
Joyce Shaughnessy

Ragnar carried the sick man to his cabin in the jungle. Upon arrival, he was surprised to see a welcoming fireplace. It reminded him of his homeland. He yearned to return there to his beloved family and friends. He didn't understand this strange place. Ragnar had grown very fond of Karlo and Kerr, but now Kerr had been taken captive by a lich—something he had never encountered in his own world. Would this never end?

The cabin was much like Roland's. Large beams stretched across the length of the ceiling, and a massive fireplace fashioned from large multi-colored stones covered the entire width of the cabin. A large pallet covered in braided cloths lay beside the fireplace. Ragnar placed the shivering man there, hoping that he would wake soon. He stared down at the sleep-tossed man and wondered how he had come to live in this strange cosmos where liches, goblins, and all manner of creatures also resided.

Karlo searched through the pantries and found sustenance enough for the two of them. As they ate, Ragnar asked, "How long does it take for your potion to work?"

"The woodsman must sleep at least six hours. Let him rest, and then we'll see."

"We must find a way to free Kerr from the clutches of the lich."

"Thank you, kind sir, for your concern for my young apprentice. I cannot imagine the evil place in which he is imprisoned. At least he is carrying the sacred beetle. If the boneman hasn't taken it away... if Kerr's soul has not already been taken." The two friends looked at each other, and there was fear in Karlo's eyes. He said wearily, "I must close my eyes for a while."

Ragnar agreed. The companions lay sleepily on pallets resting on the floor. All three dwellers in the small cabin slept.

Ragnar and Karlo woke to the sound of moaning from a corner of the room.

Karlo jumped from his bed to assist the woodsman when they heard an insistent knocking at the door. Ragnar strode purposely across the room and pulled the heavy wooden door aside. Before him stood the strangest looking creature he had yet to see in this world! He was small with pointed ears protruding from the sides of his head, and he had two horns just above each ear. He had a long skinny tail, and his skin reminded Ragnar of the lizards Karlo had informed him could change colors to adapt to their surroundings when angry or friendly. This creature was a beautiful mixture of bright green and purple. He was standing upright on two very short legs. As shocked as Ragnar was at the appearance of this lizard-like being before him, the creature looked just as surprised.

"So the rumors are true! You are the tall man here to help us fight the evil spirits that plague our world. What manner of specimen are you?"

"I am a human, of course. My name is Ragnar, and what manner of animal are you?"

"Forgive me for not introducing myself. My name is Calyptro. I am a Goblin Scout. I've come to help you and your friends on your quest."

"Our quest? Do you mean our quest to summon Ahmad or do you mean our search for his nephew?" Ragnar asked.

"I am here to help you free your friend and to guide you to your final battle, sir. May I come in? I assure you, I wish you no harm."

"Of course. Please, come in." Ragnar opened the door and welcomed the goblin into the cabin. *I must be dreaming,* thought Ragnar.

The goblin walked in. He lifted his tail to better seat himself in the chair and sat with one graceful movement. He crossed his short legs and tiny arms settling in the chair.

Ragnar said, "Have you eaten? Would you like something?"

Calyptro rubbed the underside of his belly with one of his tiny arms and said, "Oh, no thank you, sir. I have just eaten."

"Who sent you to us? I don't understand," Ragnar said.

"Horgoth Anvilstriker is a close friend of mine, and when he learned of your misfortunate encounter with the boneman, I decided that perhaps I might be of some assistance."

Just then Karlo announced, "The woodsman is waking, but he needs to rest."

Calyptro introduced himself to Karlo and said, "The one waking is a human, correct?"

Karlo nodded yes. "But he is not the Sandman."

"How odd that there are three humans in the jungle," Calyptro said.

"My name is Woldar," the woodsman woke up and coughed. "I can't remember last night. But you... carried me to my cabin. You gave me herbs..."

Ragnar asked him, "How is it that you are here? I met only one other human, and he fell into this world just as I did."

Woldar was weak. "I... came here by some misfortune. I was fighting in a war between two English kings. I rode many miles to carry a message when the earth opened before me. I was thrown from my horse, and I woke here in this jungle. I've been the only human living here for many years. I made a life in the jungle."

Ragnar asked him, "Haven't you been lonely? Haven't you yearned to go back to England?"

"Sometimes, of course, but I have found a friend. Kylo! Come here!" Woldar coughed. A monkey quickly appeared on the ledge of an open window, looking and sounding much like Capin from Roland's hut.

"This is Kylo. He has been my only companion," Woldar said.

"And no evil beings have threatened you?"

"Evil? Why, yes. But I have heard tales about two humans from far-away lands, who would someday come to this world, and I am grateful that you have finally arrived." Woldar coughed again. "Welcome to my home."

"Woldar," instructed Karlo, "you need to rest. You don't look well."

Calyptro said, "When I learned that the young dwarf had been taken, I knew that you could use my assistance."

Karlo said, "What assistance?"

"I can give you a stone—a stone that will fool the lich who holds Jesper and Kerr captive. For a short while, he will think it is the real soul gem—perhaps long enough for you to prepare for your final battle alongside the sandman."

Ragnar asked, "Who fashioned such a stone? Where did you find it?"

"I came upon an ancient wizard in the forest not far from Hogarth's cabin. He took me to see Horgoth. The wizard instructed Horgarth to make a stone. He informed us that the spell on the stone would last four days and nights. I travelled all last night to reach you. We have four days and three nights left to free Jesper and Kerr.

"Horgoth informs me that it is your destiny to free Jesper and Kerr from the clutches of evil. Otherwise the evil lich will force Jesper to make another soul gem. Once you have freed Jesper and Kerr, you must hurry on your journey to summon the Sandman and then to your final battle with the dragons. Unfortunately, the liches will have learned of our trickery well before then and will gladly join forces with the dark dragons to impede you. Never doubt one thing—you and the Sandman will be fighting not only for your lives, but also for your very souls."

"How can we be certain the lich will free them if we bargain with them, or for that matter, how can we be certain the lich hasn't already turned them into empty souls?" Karlo asked.

Calyptro said, "We have to try, don't we? We have nothing to lose."

Ragnar stood and grabbed his axe and bow and quiver. "You're right. We have to leave now." He looked at Karlo and asked, "Do you think we can find the way back to the lich's lair?"

Karlo answered, "We have to try, don't we?"

Calyptro said, "I know the way. I can assist you."

23

City of the Dead

by
H. M. Schuldt

A faint light was enough for two friends to see thick dirt walls from the third root of the mighty ash tree, Yggdrasil. They were trapped among complex rooted systems branching through dirt and air making it impossible for the dvergar to force an escape. Kerr tried many times to push against a wooded slab, but it remained secure. It had to be opened by a lich guard who banged a hammer on a metal hinge.

Down in the world of Nodhogrr, the two new friends heard a nibbling and peeling not too far away. Strange underground sounds continued, sounds that young Kerr had never heard before. A constant dull groan resonated throughout the entire root system. Underground Kerr thought the creak came from wooded vines rubbing against one another, but nothing moved. There was no wind, no breeze floating down the dirt tunnels, only stagnant air expanding into every nook and burrow where trapped victims waited for the next life, a terrible life in the city of the dead. Repetitive gnawing continued to bother Kerr as he imagined a large rat somewhere above.

"There is no way to get a good night's sleep while in captivity," Jesper explained to Kerr. "The Lich King wants us alive, and we need sharp wits."

It helped Jesper a great deal to know that the Lich King wanted them alive. Even though the dvergr jeweler was being held as a prisoner, he had some time to figure out an escape. Whenever he heard a scream from other trapped victims who had limbs devoured by the terrible serpent, Dinhogg the Corpse Ripper, he retreated to singing his charm songs. Serpents slithered down dirt passageways and weaved among mangled roots where they encircled tight wooded vines deviously waiting for their next victim.

The sacred scarab beetle slowly scanned the perimeter of the small dirt cell where Kerr stood on a slanted landing. It was as if the beetle searched for something—a way out most likely.

A slow hunched over boneman traveled alone down a tall grimy tunnel. He stopped at Jesper's cell offering mushed up food. Jesper took what he could, but only ate half of it. This hunched over boneman gave the same food to young Kerr. He thought it tasted like burnt bananas.

"Negotiate with the Lich King?" Jesper asked. "Heh! He does not meet anyone half way."

Kerr was desperate to come up with a plan, but found that he was left wanting.

"If you find a way out, you must go," Jesper said.

"I'm not leaving without you, my friend," Kerr stated.

It was young Kerr who taught Jesper a song that he learned from Ragnar. The Northman had taught Kerr this song, and since the melody sounded familiar, it was easy for Kerr to remember. Kerr had heard the melody before, but without words, when he lived back in the mines of Davlin. It brought them comfort, and Kerr knew it would fill them with just the right amount of hope they needed to get through this soiled captivity.

This will pass, we shall see light again,
Soon we'll soar high above,
Rise up, rise up, our heart in a blaze,
My enemy softens his blade.
He'll be stuck in a whirl, an unending whirl,
Our love will grow strong,
By the word of Odin.
He will set us free from this bind.
Blessed Odin come soon and
Make us anew, as a pearl shining on the shore.
We shall see the sun, we shall soar high in the sky,
Set our heart on fire and show us the way,
Break the lock, bring the key,
Victory is from Odin today.

As they sang, the scarab beetle moved faster and faster around in a circle, glowing bright.

"Pray to Odin, my friend Kerr, pray! We need to keep sharp wits!" Jesper urged.

"I'm praying!" Kerr wanted to do his part. "Blessed Odin, take pity on us and save us from this trap!"

Airy tree roots began to snap and shift. A small scruffy squirrel scurried down from on high and murmured. "The roots of Nodhogrr move at your request. You must be quick before the serpent returns."

"Prisoners!" A prisoner yelled out, fearing another victim would be taken barefoot into the horrible city of the dead. "Put on your shoes!"

A large group of slimy bonemen clanked down the dirt tunnel, passing by Kerr and Jesper. Spine-chilling liches looked as though they needed a good wash. They had a constant drool of spit and filth hanging down from their skulls. Each had a boney structure covered with random bits of fur and metal. They stopped in front of another trapped victim, banged a hammer, and opened his door. Off they took the poor victim to the city of the dead where sharp pebbles and stones stabbed at the sole of the foot.

Along Kerr's wall packed with wooded vines, a shift began to occur spreading wide among the roots. Kerr saw a way out. He led Jesper up through what seemed like a root maze that had no end. It was a tight fit, but Kerr pulled himself up higher and higher following the beetle.

"My leg is stinging!" Jesper called out as he made his way up. "It's a leech!" He pulled the sucker off and threw it down. Something fell on Jesper's head, and he hoped it wasn't another wet leech. Climbing up after Kerr, Jesper was dumbstruck entering into a haunted darkness, but he made his arms pull himself up. It began to get darker, the higher they climbed, and Jesper could not see what fell on his head. Then a loud pounding sound came from up above, and the walls shook hard.

Dirt, stop falling! Kerr thought. He called out to Jesper. "Something is pounding near the tree up above." He heard a hissing sound and knew the threat of a serpent was close by.

The beetle began to glow bright red lighting up the tunnel. Jesper saw a frightening serpent slithering toward him. It hissed again with its mouth wide open showing its venomous fangs. Within seconds wet leeches swarmed and squirmed and attached to the terrible serpent, paralyzing the predator.

Jesper and Kerr continued to climb up and up away from the serpent as more dirt came loose falling on their head. The beetle's glow began to fade, and darkness set in once again.

"I feel a tunnel on the left," Kerr said. He crawled down a long way and came to a soft pile of something. Reaching forward, he felt a slab of wood. It had a knob. Kerr pulled it open as light, heat, and delicious smells filled the tunnel. They heard water boiling and a fire crackling and were dazzled by a beautiful raging furnace inside a cozy little burrow. An ugly little goblin approached with a dagger ready to fight.

"We come in peace! We were taken by the Lich King as prisoners, and we have found a way out," Kerr said. He looked down and saw his boots standing on a big pile of compost.

"Greetings! Welcome to my Clay Scullery. It is terrible down there, now isn't it? Come quickly! And don't ruin my compost! I am Barry who lives under the Rose Bay." A strange little goblin squinted his small beady eyes and viewed his three guests. He threw a bucket of worms out the door and carefully shut the oval slab. His scrunched up fat little body showed the way to a wood table. His voice rattled as he spoke. "My, that is the biggest beetle I've ever seen."

"We are on our way to see our friend," Kerr said peering down the hall. "Let us pass through and be on our way."

Dishes and pans rattled as the burrow shook again.

"Eat and drink with me first, and let me tell you some bad news," Barry said. He climbed upon a bench. "We need to hide from a Jotun. You might know him as a frost giant. He has brought a terrible storm into our land. He is in big trouble for losing the Lich King's sword. He leaves behind a terrible chill that kills trees and plants and creatures like you and me. You are welcome to stay here until the Jotun has moved on."

Jesper and Kerr were happy to stay for a short while and fill up on roasted potato wedges spiced with onion, garlic, and rosemary. They raised horns to their mouths and drank hot wassail as they told the goblin about the terrible root world below.

"What is your skill?" Barry asked the dvergr, sitting around a small wooden table.

"I am a jeweler, maker of fine stones and all types of jewelry," Jesper said. He took another drink savoring the cinnamon and orange spice.

"And you?" Barry asked Kerr. He raised his eyebrowless eyebrows and flared his pale nostrils.

"I am a Master Climber and a Fine Musician," Kerr stated.

"Your climbing skill came in handy today," Barry said, using his stubby fingers to grasp onto his horn. He lifted it high and took another drink of hot wassail. "What instrument do you play?"

"The piccolo," Kerr answered. He often played alone when no one could bother him. It often attracted the owls.

"'Tis true," Jesper said. "And your charm song may have well saved our lives. Let me guess your skill, my little goblin friend. You're a Master Cook."

"Have you ever tasted better potatoes?" Barry asked.

They heard voices down another passageway. Barry referred to the noise as *those pesky little goblins*, which was most certainly odd since he was a goblin himself, and he assured his new friends they were not in danger for the time being. After several clanks and bangs and shouts from down the way, Barry asked Kerr to play his instrument. Kerr took out his piccolo and began playing a soothing melody. Somewhere up above, an owl flew near and sat upon a low branch near the Rose Bay above Barry's home.

24

Tombstone

by
Randall Lemon

After a time, the noise down the passageway ceased, but it put Kerr and Jesper on edge. They appreciated Barry's hospitality and understood the necessity of waiting out the frost giant who stormed around outside Barry's hut, near the tree whose root system had formed the basis for the prison from which they had so recently escaped. Kerr could not help but be nervous and anxious to be on his way.

"My friends, if that giant does not leave soon, I fear we will have to attempt running by it. Barry, you have been an excellent host. But if some of the lich minions explore our cell, they will soon find the tunnel that opened to allow us to escape. That tunnel leads right up here to your compost heap, Barry. I fear that Jesper and I have put you in danger."

Barry suddenly appeared quite alarmed, "I can see that you are right, Kerr. Do you have any musical charm that can draw the giant away from us? Or is there some way you can utilize the wondrous abilities of your scarab beetle to get us out of this fix?"

Kerr responded sadly, "I am afraid I have nothing that will supply us with such a miracle. If my friend, Ragnar were here, he might be able to slay the giant with his champion axe, but even that would be a prodigious feat. I think we will have to rely on our intelligence to supply us with a way of escape. What do we know about frost giants that might aid us?"

Jesper was quick to respond. "They are enormous and extremely strong but not renowned for their intelligence. Maybe we can fool him somehow?"

Kerr thought further and said, "We know they are creatures of ice, snow, and cold. Is it not logical that they may fear or be weakened by fire and heat?"

Barry was quick to take up the thread, "I believe I understand what you are suggesting. My hut is built right under the Rose Bay near the base of this mighty tree. As you know I am a cook of some renown, so I have all manner of kindling to make my fires and oils that I use in my cooking. Since it appears that at any moment the evil liches and his cohorts might overrun my hut as they search for you, it might be an easy task to start my hut on fire. We can dig into the compost heap and hide there until our small fire becomes a raging conflagration. Hopefully the burning hut will drive the Jotun from the area, and we can make our escape and get as far as possible from here before anyone is the wiser."

So the three small creatures put their desperate plan into action spreading oil and kindling throughout the hut and preparing to light the hut afire, hoping the liches and serpents would stay away. One of the pesky little goblins marched right up to Kerr and gave him a slender shaft made out of wood from the mighty Yggdrasil. "Take this relic of great power and use it to free your people and ours." Then the twelve little goblins scurried upstairs as Barry began to light the hut on fire.

The entrance to Barry's hut blazed brightly just as they had hoped while twelve pesky little goblins sat in the Rose Bay taking notice from afar. The sight of this fire caused the frost giant to bellow fearfully, and the twelve little goblins began to scatter. The giant ran from the area of the flames knowing he was particularly vulnerable to damage from fire. He caught one of the goblins and smashing the small goblin's body into a sickening paste, swallowed him in one gulp.

Once they heard the stomping giant flee, Barry popped his head out of the compost heap and hardly recognized his kitchen. Sadly walking through soot and hot coals, the creatures made their way to daylight. Barry stayed with Kerr and Jesper while the rest of the pesky little goblins scurried off into the dense forest.

***

Ragnar and Karlo were consulting with Calyptro about what they could do to rescue Karlo's young nephew, Kerr.

Ragnar knew he had to hearten the flagging spirits of Karlo. "Karlo, my friend, I do not think that we should fear so much for the life of Kerr. In the short time I have known him, I have found him to be both brave and ingenious. Plus, do not forget that he has the scarab beetle with him. Added to that is the fact that the lich took him prisoner when he probably could have easily killed him if that was his intent. Too long we have allowed ourselves to be pursued by this monster or that. Now I say it is time we stopped being the prey and become instead the hunters. Let us concentrate on where and how we can find the place the lich is holding him."

Karlo looked at Ragnar with tears of appreciation in his eyes, "You are right, my good friend Ragnar. We will not give up my nephew without a fight. Calyptro, you are more familiar with the area hereabouts than Ragnar or myself. What can you offer that might help us?"

The goblin and woodsman conferred for a couple of moments suggesting and rejecting various ideas. Woldar shifted in his chair, obviously weak from his ordeal with jungle poison. He was also quite morose because he began to believe he would never see his beloved England again.

Finally Calyptro seemed to have reached a decision. "I have come up with a good plan to help you find your apprenticed nephew. I have roamed these woods all my life, and during that time I have found a wide variety of strange places. I will tell you about one of them, but Woldar is too weak from jungle fever to take you there. I know where to go, and I will be able to guide you, but I must be honest. All those who have helped you will be put into mortal danger if we fail in our quest."

Woldar coughed. "Since you and the Sandman arrived here, I have wanted to find you. After this is all over, if you find out how to return yourselves to your worlds, come back here... and take me with you."

Ragnar put both hands on the blade of his axe. "You did not even have to ask this Woldar, for this is something I would willingly do as I am sure would Ahmad. For your peace of mind, I swear to you by All-Father Odin, most mighty that I will not forget the boon of your aid. When we discover the secret of how to return, we will come back to take you with us. If I break this promise, let my place in Valhalla be taken away and may my soul be consigned to the oblivion of Hel for all time."

Karlo edged forward in his seat, "So, how can you help us?"

Calyptro once again rubbed the area of his underbelly and launched into a narrative. "There is an ancient cemetery hidden in the depths of these woods. In it, hidden beneath a certain tombstone, is a secret gate that opens into a tunnel. This tunnel runs straight and true to the mighty ash tree, Yggdrasil. It is there where we believe the Lich King and his underlings make their lair. It is most likely there you will find your nephew and any other prisoners the lich holds captive. Perhaps when we arrive you can trick the Lich King into taking the counterfeit soul gem gifted to us by the ancient wizard as ransom for Kerr. But after that we will have to act quickly to get as far away from the liches as possible. Once the Lich King discovers our ruse, his anger will be fearsome to behold."

Gathering their equipment, Ragnar and Karlo set off with Calyptro leading the way. Deeper and deeper into the dark forest the trio delved. The going was not easy and often Ragnar had to use his axe to free their paths of the creeper vines that clogged it. Finally Calyptro let out a yelp. Ragnar and Karlo gripped their weapons preparing to fight some new menace, but Calyptro quickly assured them that he had just stumbled into one of the stones that still stood as a tumbledown wall around the cemetery for which they had aimed.

"Just barked my shin is all," said Calyptro. "Now we will need to find the correct tombstone that hides the secret gate into the tunnel."

Most of the stones were old and had long since been tumbled or eroded by the passage to centuries. Taking his bearings, Calyptro moved in the direction he believed the singular tombstone indicated by Woldar would lie. He stopped a few times and once even retraced his steps. But finally he indicated a massive tombstone overgown with weeds and vines and ivy.

"We will need to clear the area at the base of the stone. It may take a little digging, but Woldar said we will find the gate here and the tunnel beyond it." The three immediately began working clearing underbrush from the tombstone itself and the area around it. Finally it was cleared, but nothing unusual was revealed.

"There is no gate here," groused Ragnar.

"Wait my friend, Woldar told me the trick involved. I merely need to grasp the tombstone and turn it around. Through some deviltry, it will spin. If it does, the gate will open," Calyptro said.

Calyptro tried with all his might, but he was not strong enough by himself to turn the ancient stone and open the way. So Ragnar gripped the massive stone in his large hands. The sinews and veins along his shoulders and arms popped out as he strained and finally turned the tombstone completely around. A gate opened in the ground, and Karlo and Calyptro prepared to move through it into the tunnel. That is when they noticed that Ragnar appeared frozen in place staring at the tombstone. The hair on his head and arms was standing straight up as he looked at the inscription on the newly revealed front of the tombstone.

Karlo placed his hand on the Viking's arm. "What is wrong my friend? We must move quickly if we are to save Kerr."

His eyes wide and his breathing shallow, Ragnar raised an arm and pointed to the inscription on the tombstone. "By Odin's beard!! What evil is this?"

For the first time, Karlo looked at the face of the tombstone. On it was written one word, "R-A-G-N-A-R."

25

A Rattling Voice

by
Lynette White

"It is a trick, you fools!" Calyptro yelled. "The moment you turn the stone, he knows who is coming for him. If we stand here long enough, the gate will close. We'll lose not only our chance to save Kerr, but we'll draw the liches to us. The only chance we have is to keep moving so he can not pin us down."

Calyptro's sharp warning was enough for Ragnar to focus on the moment. It did little, however, to shake the impending doom penetrating down to the root of his soul.

Calyptro scrambled down into the tunnel, and Ragnar stumbled after him. Karlo hesitated for a moment before following them inside. They stopped as the stagnant air of death assaulted them. Even the very dirt reeked of death.

"Where do we go from here?" Karlo whispered.

The sound of rustling and a flint striking echoed off the dirt walls. Ragnar and Karlo were forced to cover their eyes as a torch flared to life. Calyptro pointed down a dark tunnel.

"That way." He remarked sarcastically and started to lead them down the tunnel. "But we must move quickly. We must find Kerr and Jesper before the Lich King finds us."

Ragnar drew his axe with a sigh. "Of course we do. Why would I expect anything different?" He moaned.

***

Kerr and his companions absentmindedly followed the scarab as it led them deeper into the forest. They could hear the frost giant crashing through the forest howling in a blind rage.

They had not gone far when the beetle suddenly stopped and began to click furiously. They barely kept their feet beneath them and avoided stepping on the beetle as it frantically started running in a circle around them.

The beetle's iridescent colors grew brighter with each revolution until it formed a perfect circle of light around them.

"What is it doing, Kerr?" Jesper whispered.

Kerr shrugged and shook his head while dreading the unknown threat, but Barry sucked in his breath, gasping loudly.

Kerr and Jesper spun around to see what had frightened Barry.

"Holy gods!" Kerr panted.

A cloud of darkness moved toward them. Their minds and bodies were paralyzed with fear. Kerr tried to focus on the clicking sound coming from the beetle, but his mind refused to fight the overpowering fear.

A voice rattled from the darkness. "You fools think you can escape from me? Prepare to serve me for eternity!"

Kerr thought his heart was going to burst from terror and he was helpless to stop it. They would die here without a fight. A part of him refused to give up, however, and his brain finally locked onto the clicking. The fear gradually turned to rage. He shouted, "No! I will never serve you!"

The Lich King's laugh was bone chilling. "Oh, but you will, Kerr." It corrected him, and a bony finger appeared out of the darkness.

Lightening crackled in a black cloud surrounding the evil king and then shot through his outstretched finger. The killing blast skidded off the invisible barrier, exploding a tree behind the trio.

"What treachery is this?" The lich roared.

Kerr had closed his eyes and prepared to die, but his eyes popped open when the tree exploded behind them. He instinctively covered his head with his arms as the debris fell around them, but nothing touched them.

Kerr's eyes went to the lich then behind him, and to the crashing trees. The lich spun around as the trees immediately behind him shattered. The frost giant crashed through, blinded by his senseless tree smashing. The lich had to turn his attention away from his prey to subdue his minion.

"Stop you fool!"

Kerr's attention went back to his feet. The scarab's clicking was urgent, and his carapace glowed red. It ran into the brush, and Kerr started after him. He shouted to the others. "Move it!"

They followed the scarab into the forest and never hesitated when it suddenly led them into a tunnel.

***

Ragnar walked directly behind Calyptro as they made their way through the tunnels. They made no effort to keep their presence a secret any longer. A trail of undead bodies left by Ragnar's axe declared their every step.

They heard footsteps rushing toward them and pressed themselves against the wall. Ragnar and Karlo heard the distinctive clicking sound at the same time and exchanged smiles. They spoke together, "Kerr."

Ragnar stepped past Calyptro. "Kerr, is that you? We are here! Keep coming toward us." He announced down the tunnel.

The footsteps stopped. "Ragnar!" Kerr yelled back.

"Yes, Kerr. I am with Karlo. Follow my voice. Is Jesper with you?"

"Yes, he is with me." Kerr answered.

A moment later the scarab's red glow came around a corner, and right behind it were Kerr, Jesper, and Barry. Karlo rushed past Calyptro and ran to his nephew. They slid into each other's open arms.

Ragnar scooped both of them into his large arms. "Thank Odin you are safe, Kerr."

"This is all touching, but what if he is one of them now?" Calyptro challenged.

Karlo pointed at the beetle. "If he was then he would not be protected by the sacred scarab."

Kerr broke away. "Uncle is right. The scarab protected us but we must flee! The Lich King is hunting us. We just barely escaped him. We scared the frost giant when we set Barry's hut on fire. He stumbled across us, and the scarab led us back here to find you." He tumbled out before taking a breath.

"Whoa, little one." Ragnar stopped him. "You can tell me later. Calyptro, get us out of here."

They rushed back up the tunnel and out the gate. Ragnar stopped in his tracks when he popped out of the tunnel. The Lich King had left him a message on the tombstone:

Ragnar,

> *You will never see the Sword Master again and you cannot defeat me alone.*

26

𝔄 𝕯𝖊𝖆𝖉𝖑𝖞 𝕮𝖍𝖎𝖑𝖑

by

Christian Warren Freed

"Stop," Hygliak whispered. His hand held up in a clenched fist. The goblin lowered his spear and squatted. "We are not alone."

Ahmad exhaled slowly. He was tired, and he wanted to return to his land—and his time. Senses on overload, the Saracen drew his sword and prepared to battle. Again his soft, brown eyes scanned the immediate area and found nothing. They reached an edge of the desert. Sand gradually gave way to scrub brush and a light scattering of trees.

"What do you see?" Ahmad asked.

The goblin edged forward. His head cocked as he listened to the sounds of the approaching forest. "I cannot tell. There is magic at work here. We are deep in the Lich King's territory. Trust nothing. Believe nothing. It is the only way to survive."

Ahmad tensed reflexively. Thus far he had no reason to doubt Hygliak. The goblin had steered him right from the moment they met. Their bond was not strong, but it grew deeper the longer they spent on the road. He found himself wanting to meet the king and his army. He wanted to find out how they planned on defeating the lich. More than this, he wanted to find a way home.

"I don't see anything," Ahmad said. "Are you sure we are being watched?"

Hygliak turned and stared at him. "Watched? We're being hunted."

The implications sent chills down him. Ahmad glanced at Rostok. The mighty gryffon ducked its head and shook softly. *Even the gryffon knows we're being hunted*, Ahmad thought. *What have I gotten myself into this time?*

"Perhaps we should turn back?" Ahmad suggested.

Hygliak disagreed. "It is too late for that. The Lich King won't let us leave. Our only option is to forge ahead and confront whatever foul machinations await us."

Thunder rumbled across the skies. Dark clouds swarmed in, blotting out the punishing sun. Ahmad listened to a hiss-splatter coming from the sands behind him. His eyes widened in shock as he turned and saw steam rising from the sand. The very grains seemed to melt when struck.

"This is no ordinary storm," Hygliak balked.

"That's not rain. It's acid. We'll be burnt to the bone if we're caught in the open. Run! Into the forest!" Ahmad said. Only then did he realize the thick canopy wouldn't allow the gryffon a chance to fly, drastically reducing his capabilities. "You must fly," he urged Rostok. "Flee while you still can!"

Rostok looked first to the goblin and then back to Ahmad. Understanding filled its eyes. With a flap of mighty wings, the gryffon leapt off the ground. Ahmad knew they would meet again on the far side of the forest.

He and Hygliak ran as fast as their weary legs would take them, certain that death stalked them. Small trees and bushes caught flame and melted. The very ground seemed to scream a low, torturous cry. Gradually the forest thickened. Trees were larger and became taller. Eventually the canopy thickened enough to prevent the acidic rain from penetrating. They were safe for the time being.

Man and goblin wandered deeper into the forest, following a small deer path. They remained on guard, despite there being no evidence of anything in the area. Ahmad lost track of time. They walked and walked until coming to a small clearing where they halted.

"What happened here?" Ahmad asked. Dozens of trees were broken, seemingly burst from the inside out. Branches and trunks lay scattered across the ground. Other branches looked peeled. A dread feeling entered him. He had seen this before, but where? "Hygliak, we must find a way out of here. We are…"

Heavy footsteps shook the ground, knocking the goblin down. His eyes widened. Never before had he experienced anything of the sort. Ahmad glimpsed frozen images of something through the trees. He winced and steadied his nerves when he saw an arm—powerful legs—a pure white beard and those horns protruding from a skull. Just meters away, a frost giant emerged into the clear.

The frost giant bellowed. Bits of chewed flesh and phlegm spewed from its mouth. Ice colored eyes stared down on Ahmad with unadulterated hatred. The giant remembered. He spread his arms wide and drew them together with a terrible thunderclap. Nearby trees shattered. Splinters sliced through the air like arrows. A column of ice and snow burst from its hands to attack Ahmad.

Bracing himself Ahmad failed to notice Hygliak charge from the side. The goblin scout knocked Ahmad out of the blast an instant before it struck. Hygliak was not so fortunate. The frost giant's attack caught him squarely in the chest. The goblin had time to turn his head and give Ahmad a knowing look filled with horror as his body was slowly consumed by ice.

"Hygliak!" Ahmad screamed.

The frost giant roared again. Vibrations pulsed into the goblin, shattering him into thousands of ice crystals. Ahmad stared at the remains, unsure of what happened or why. He was torn between the desire either to kill the giant or to flee. Even with the powerful sword, he knew he lacked the courage to win. Nor did he want to waste Hygliak's sacrifice.

Rolling to his feet, the Saracen leveled his sword at the frost giant. "You shall pay for this, you monster!"

The frost giant laughed.

27

Dragon Toe

by
Joyce Shaughnessy

Anger rose up in Ahmad—an anger he could not control. He had been threatened by one horrible demon after another. Now this stupid cruel monster had taken the life of Hygliac, whom he had grown to respect and admire as a friend.

Pointing his sword at the mighty beast, he prayed that the sword would defeat his foe. Standing before the massive frost giant, he screamed, "I swear by the Prophet Muhammed that this will be the last time you take another life! The goodness and power of my sword shall take you from this world!"

Ahmad thought for a moment that the magic hadn't worked when a massive frigid cold came blasting toward him from the giant's breath. But before it reached his body, the giant's chilling exhale dissolved. And at that moment, a cloud of hot steam burst forth from the tip of the sword flying up into the open mouth of the frost giant. Placing his hands up to his face, the giant wailed in a mournful cry— he stomped so powerfully that it shook the ground. Then he turned and immediately dissolved into millions of tiny ice crystals. If Ahmad had been any closer he would have been covered in them.

Sinking onto his knees, he recited a solemn Muslim prayer of mourning for Hygliac. Then he rose and started to walk in the jungle, hoping to find his way to Rostok, but he did not know where to go next. Soon he came upon a river. After walking a few miles, he met a strange little man who was pulling a small rowboat onto shore.

As Ahmad got closer, he was amazed at the sight. The little man was literally one layer of wrinkles upon another. There was neither a beginning nor an end to each level of folds.

The small man saw Ahmad and gasped in shock. "Well, you have finally arrived, the Sandman who will lift the curse that makes our land suffer. I've heard the tales of your coming for decades, but I had given up hope that you would appear in my lifetime." The man gathered his wits and said, "I beg your pardon, sir, I failed to introduce myself. I am known as Selflara the Ancient One. I wonder—I heard an enormous moaning from far away. It sounded much like a wounded beast. Were you a part of that?"

Ahmad exhaled. "I suppose I was. You knew I was coming?"

"Oh, yes. We knew that *you and the Northman* would come eventually, but I had no idea it would be today. And by what name should I call you?"

"My name is Ahmad-Ibn Fazzat."

"Welcome, my friend. If you should so require, I can transport you further down the river. It flows swiftly."

"I have no means with which to pay you for your services."

"No need. It is an honor to serve you."

It was Ahmad who first felt the relief of blowing wind in the humid air. They had traveled down the river and out of the forest's cover when Ahmad heard the joyous beating of Rostok's majestic wings. "Selfara, stop! And pull to shore!"

Rostok appeared and landed gracefully. He gave his master a friendly look with deep black eyes. Ahmad came to shore, and the gryffon knelt in submission. As Ahmad bid Selfara goodbye, Rostok took him to the skies above the jungle canopy. Ahmad didn't know where the gryffon would carry him, but he knew that through comradeship, they would find Ragnar.

***

An unlikely group of travelers—Ragnar, Karlo, Calyptro, Jesper, Barry, and Kerr with his beetle—slowly made their way through the jungle. Calyptro feared at each turn that the evil boneman would greet them. As they made their way to Barry's hut, which was now only a sodden mass of blackened twigs, they could smell the lingering odor of ash.

Ragnar stared at the enormous Yggdrasil Tree, amazed that it had put out the blazing fire. He muttered, "I don't believe it. Look! Leaves on the tree turned upside down. Magical leaves... must have directed the rain to extinguish the fire. If I hadn't seen it with my own two eyes, I would not have believed it! It truly is a miracle."

Calyptro nervously hastened them on, knowing that the spell placed on the false soul gem would only last two more days. If they should come upon the Lich King, it would be the only bargaining tool they possessed.

"Something is astir, Ragnar. Even the beetle feels it."

Suddenly they heard a roar—the roar of a mighty black dragon. *Where is it?* Ragnar stood ready to fight. Dragon fire caused the dark canopy to light up. It was upon them in seconds. The others, except for the scarab, hid behind Ragnar hoping that he could slay the dragon with his champion axe. Ragnar strode so close to the dragon that he could smell the creature's foul fire breath. Fireproof armor made by Horgoth Anvilstriker kept him safe.

Once upon the dragon, Ragnar skillfully used his axe to cut through the dragon's flesh. It fell writhing on the ground in pain. Approaching the dragon with quiet legs, the beetle stopped and began to click with his carapace rising up and down. Ragnar knew that his only hope of slowing the dragon down was to chop off one of its toes but which one? The beetle knew all too well which toe held the power of a black dragon's eyesight, and so he ran near the offending toe. Ragnar once again wielded his weapon, and he skillfully chopped off a toe.

The dragon emitted such a mournful cry that it could be heard for miles. A conflagration caused by his terrible fire breath continued to light up the jungle cover, but the dragon was instantly blinded, and he became very angry.

"Make a run for it!" Ragnar shouted, as he knelt down long enough to bag up the offending toe. They quickly fled into the trees knowing that the dragon was not their only threat. They would soon meet the Lich King. Their only hope was still in the false soul gem that Calyptro carried.

The men continued on through the trees running for their lives when they came upon another awful sound. This time they heard a shrilling cry of scorn closing in on them from all around. It was the sound of deceitful laughter, and it carried a stench—the promise of eternal death. Ragnar assumed his fighting position while Kerr turned in dread, and an evil Djinn said, "Prepare to meet your doom, oh, mortal ones. You will not escape me this time!"

28

Trapped In Mud

by

H. M. Schuldt

Ragnar felt the summoning stone thrum warmly on his chest. He knew Ahmad must be close by in this section of the swampy jungle where ground-dwelling animals scurried about.

***

"Tell me! Tell me! Why you are after us!" Kerr shouted to the Reptile Djinn. "For the life of me, I can't see anything we have done to deserve your wrath!"

Ragnar prepared for an attack keeping his eyes on the three slithering tails. These extremities towered above Kerr, forcing him into a muddy place near an old rock wall. Blue fire sparked from the ends of four scaly arms. The creature's lightning speed and strength could outdo any human or dvergr. Without feet, the Reptile Djinn hovered mysteriously into the air. Three coils of dry scaly skin circled from his haunches, around his puffed up chest, and loosely around his neck as if it were a scarf. It continued into three reptilian tails out from his head. He lashed at Kerr and missed.

"It is not worth teaching you, little man-child. Prepare to die!" The cold-blooded djinn hissed at Kerr. Four sinuous arms flailed out toward Kerr, placing Kerr in the sinking mud. Showing his lizard teeth, the foul-tempered djinn hovered in front of the old rock wall.

Sitting on the edge of the muddy spot, the scarab beetle remained still without lighting up.

Ragnar appeared. "You owe us an explanation," he sneered, and then lightning flashed. Ragnar knew the power of Odin's throne was on his side. "You chase us, and we do not know why. We have friends hiding in the trees watching you as witnesses. They will send a message to the Djinn Vultures, and my friends will tell your clergy how you failed to state your reason. Your leaders will punish you and throw you into the eternal pit of torment for being a coward. You'll be labeled a dishonorable fighter unless you speak now and tell us why you hunt us down. Tell us now or meet your doom!"

"Enough! I am eternal. You cannot kill me," smirked the Djinn. Thunder was heard off in the distance. His lower jaw quivered, fearing his own clergy. "I have been sent to take Ahmad Ibn Fazzat out of this terrible land. He killed one of our dragons, and he must pay for his crime. A gryffon has brought him here on account of you. It is your fault he has come to this place. Before I can take him, I must get rid of you!"

"Not so," Karlo said. "Ahmad has been sent here by powers greater than you, from the ancient throne on high. Ahmad has the duty to bring us something, and it will happen according to prophecy. No matter how much blood you spill, there is nothing any of us can do to stop Ahmad's return. But there has been a mistake. Ahmad took a weapon that does not belong to him. All we need is the weapon he carries. Once we receive it, Ahmad is free to leave."

"So you see," added Kerr, his legs sinking further into the muddy spot, "if you shed innocent blood, your leaders will send you to the eternal pit of torment where you will suffer day and night."

"You cannot trick me!" bellowed the Reptile Djinn as he floated over the sloshy mud in which Kerr was trapped. "My leaders sent me here to bring Ahmad back to pay for his crime."

"The hand of Odin shall come to our rescue and serve us well," Ragnar spoke confidently. A flash of lightning struck directly above. "Stall no longer, djinn. Go save your own reputation among the Djinn Vultures." Lightning cracked down hard on a tall redwood tree. The sound resonated deep in his chest. A great wind blew from the west, pushing hard against a giant tree. It came crashing down to the ground, landing over a wide hidden crack in the earth. The Reptile Djinn moved out of the way as the tree slammed down.

Looking down, Kerr noticed he was sinking. The mud was sucking him down way too quickly. He hung onto a branch and struggled to pull one foot out of the filthy suction.

Blue and green waves of energy surged from beneath the Reptile Djinn. As quick as lightning, he deserted Kerr and sped down a narrow trail.

Kerr climbed up onto the fallen redwood. He was covered in mud from the knees down. He noticed a mud nest and carefully passed by. Taking a stick, he dropped it into the ravine. After several seconds, the stick hit water, and he heard a sizzle. A wasp buzzed by and flew down into the earth's crack. Leaning over the edge of the fallen redwood, he smelled pickled red meat. He stepped carefully along the fallen tree and returned to his friends. Standing on the fallen redwood he said,

"I saw dragon eggs down in the ravine. There must be an underground water chamber close by."

"Sure they weren't stones?" Karlo asked.

"Dragon eggs, set in clear water," Kerr said.

"It must be acid water," Karlo clarified.

"How so?" Ragnar asked.

"Black dragon eggs must be submerged in strong acid water. It's where they hatch," Karlo said. "Black dragon eggs can only mean one thing. There must be a Skull Dragon close by."

"We could steal an egg to use it as a bargaining chip," Kerr chuckled.

"Not a bad idea," Ragnar said.

The fallen redwood had saved Kerr's life by the hand of Odin. It revealed the location of black dragon eggs and provided a way to reach the other side of the ravine. Plant growth hid the ravine from view. Thick swampy trees made it impossible for any dragon to fly upward, but the location was excellent for hiding dragon eggs.

29

Delfin's Formula

by
Randall Lemon

"You know what might be even better than one of the eggs," Ragnar said. "The whole nest! If we were to steal all of the eggs, they could give us the negotiating tool we need in dealing with these Skull Dragons of which you speak."

Karlo quietly answered with some concern in his voice, "It could make them hate us as well. Do you really think it wise, Ragnar?"

Most unexpectedly, a roar of laughter broke from deep within the Northman's chest. "My little friend, do you not already think that the dragons hate us? Did the Djinn not make that as clear as day? I think there is very little we can do to provoke their hatred anymore."

Karlo smiled back. "We have put great faith in you, Ragnar. And you have never let us down. So I should not question your wisdom in this matter. But how do you suggest we get them? The nest looks to be a good three feet beneath the surface of the acid. Surely if we touch the acid, we will be horribly disfigured—perhaps killed. If we reach in with your marvelous champion ax, it might be irreparably damaged. Anything else might be dissolved before it even reached the nest."

Ragnar contemplated the matter for a moment and then seemed to reach a decision. "We can climb down this ravine until we are close enough to see the nest. Something will suggest itself to us."

Using the fallen redwood to aid them in descending the steep wall of the ravine, they began making their way down. Suddenly Barry screamed and began tumbling down the wall right toward the pool of acid at the base of the ravine.

Ragnar grabbed for the goblin as he rolled by him but was unable to get hold of him. Poor Barry looked doomed to falling into acid when Kerr, who had been leading them down the way he had come, let go of the support of the redwood and threw himself full-length at Barry trying to impede his fall. For a moment they hung onto the side of the ravine. Then slowly they started to continue their slide down to almost certain death by dissolving.

Suddenly Kerr saw something sticking out from the muddy side of the ravine and caught it with one of his hands while grasping Barry's tunic with the other. The young dvergr strained trying to hold onto the heavy goblin. Veins popped out on the neck and arms of Kerr.

"Let me go," Barry cried. "You cannot hold on to us both. Save yourself. I am not needed for your quest."

"Shut up!" Kerr growled. "You helped save us from that frost giant, when you had absolutely no reason to do so. I will not let a heroic comrade die when there is still strength enough in my body to save him."

At that moment two large arms formed of mud, leaves, twigs, dirt, and dust reached out from the very side of the ravine right from the spot where Kerr hung. Startled, Kerr lost his grip but, before the two friends could fall to their death, the arms wrapped them both in an embrace. And a voice rumbled, emanating from the object onto which he had held. "Fear not, I will not let such heroism go unrewarded. You are safe in my arms. I will not let you fall."

By this time Ragnar and the three other companions had formed a human chain to where Kerr and Barry hung. A ledge began to form beneath the companions jutting out of the side of the ravine itself until there was room for six companions and one other. Dust and dirt from one corner of the ledge began to rise into the air and, as it rose, it began to form into a somewhat amorphous female shape. As tall as two men standing on each other's shoulders, the creature towered over all, even Ragnar. In its arms it held a gigantic book.

It was Kerr who spoke first, "Thank you great one for rescuing us." And Kerr tried to bow awkwardly to the huge creature. "To whom do I owe my life?"

The creature's deep and sensual voice seemed to rumble more from its chest than from its face. "In a very real way, you owe your life to yourself. As you fell, you grabbed the edge of this tome, which caused me as its guardian to become sentient once more, for I am tied to this book for all time. Once I had a name and a life of my own. I served a great alchemist, a man renowned far and wide for his skills with metals and herbs and solutions of all kinds. He discovered a formula for what he thought was the elixir vitae, which would allow him to live forever.

"But the formula was imperfect and, while it increased his lifespan, it weakened him immensely. Realizing that he would soon be unable to do things for himself and would be helpless, he asked me if I would allow him to make me into a servant that would be around to help him for all of his long life. Unlike himself, I would never lose my strength. Though he did not know it, I had long been in love with him and had no desire to ever part from him. So I allowed him to do as he wished.

"From that day to this, Eleanor the servant girl ceased to exist. I became the Dust Elemental you see today. He tied my spirit to the book that always lay at his side—the book that contained all the experiments he had attempted and all the formulae he had discovered. That way whenever he needed me, he only had to touch the book, and I would appear to do his bidding. At first I was horrified by the creature he had transformed me into, but when I cried, the dust of my body would only turn to mud. Gradually I realized that perhaps what he had done to me was a boon to us both. For each night I lay close by his side, and I would feel the warmth of his touch on me whenever he reached and lovingly stroked the cover of the book to bring me forth. It was almost like we were lovers.

"But finally came the day he died, and the townsmen wrapped us up in the blankets of his bed and carried us to the side of this ravine and rolled us down its side. They thought it fitting that a man whose whole life had been devoted to acids and bases and the like would meet his ultimate end in acid. As we rolled down the hill, the blanket became unraveled. I lay on the side of this ravine gradually being covered by mud and twigs brought down the ravine sides by the rains until only the corner of my cover stuck out from the dirt.

"Your touch has brought me out of darkness and back to this world. So it is I who should be thanking you for my life."

Calyptro's eyes seemed to glow, "Did you say that your master worked with bases and acids and wrote all his finding and formulae down in this magnificent tome? Is it possible that he might have a formula that would be able to neutralize acid?"

The dust elemental formerly known as Eleanor rumbled in response. "My Delfin was the greatest alchemist of his age. I was but a poor uneducated servant and could not read that which he wrote. If there is such a thing, I am sure it would be in Delfin's book."

Ragnar stared up at the creature, "Eleanor, would you mind if we looked through the book to see if we could find some knowledge that might aid us in our quest?"

Eleanor responded, "As long as you swear not to damage the book nor remove any of the pages, I would be glad to allow you to peruse it." With that Eleanor changed her body into steps up the side of the ravine to its top. They climbed to the top of the ravine where Karlo opened the book.

As he flipped through the pages, he suddenly stopped and stared intently.

Ragnar, tried to look over Karlo's shoulder, "Have you found it? Does that page contain the secret of neutralizing the acid in the pool that covers the skull dragon eggs?"

Karlo turned to fix his eyes on the barbarian, "No, but here is something that might help us greatly in defeating all the living minions of the lich, though it cannot harm the lich or any of his undead allies. On this page is the formula for a poisonous gas like that breathed by the green dragons, a chlorine gas. But more than that there is a diagram here of a device that one man could carry that would allow him to spread the deadly gas and a special mask he could wear that would make him invulnerable to its deadly effects."

"That is all well and good," said Ragnar. "But for now, we are seeking a solution that will protect one from the acid of the pool."

"You are never satisfied." Karlo sniffed and he continued to page through the massive tome. After ten more minutes of page turning, Karlo finally piped up excitedly. "Eureka! This should do it."

30

𝔅linded

by
Lynette White

"So speak, man! Can we do this or not?" Ragnar pushed when Karlo failed to offer any more information.

Karlo glared at Ragnar. "Of course I can do this, your mightiness." He huffed as he stood up and slid his pack off his back.

He muttered to himself as he sorted his pack, placing most of the items in one pile and a select few in another. Satisfied he found everything he needed, Karlo quickly put his things back into his pack.

"Kerr, I am going to need your help here, son."

Kerr had been anxiously waiting for those words. In all this madness he missed spending entire days in the elder dvergr's home making potions. He jumped up and was immediately at Karlo's side.

"What do you need me to do, Uncle?"

Karlo raised a finger to stall him and then focused on Ragnar. "This is going to take awhile..." He pointed at Ragnar's chest. "...so if you need to, go do what you need to do."

The stone was still warm, and Ragnar smiled knowingly. This place was far too dangerous to concentrate for very long, but he would take what time he had. He stood up.

"Thank you, my friend." He said and walked a short distance away.

"The rest of you post guard. No one is to disturb Ragnar unless there is a true threat, understood?"

Calyptro, Jesper, and Barry just nodded obediently and spread out to form a perimeter. Ragnar sat down, closed his eyes and pinched the bridge of his nose as he leaned heavily against the tree. He fought in more battles then he could count but had never been this tired or dispirited.

His mind drifted to his beloved Lagertha. He missed her so much he thought his heart would shatter. "I will be home soon, my beloved. Somehow I will find my way out of this cursed place and back to you."

With a sigh he brought forth the summoning stone and searched his exhausted mind for Roland's words.

Place the warm stone on the forehead. Concentrate on Ahmad and call upon his gryffon. Ask for their help. And do not be distracted by anything else. Roland's voice echoed.

Ragnar placed the stone against his forehead and did as Roland instructed. This time he was not going to fail.

***

Rostok suddenly bucked, so Ahmad tightened his hold on the reigns. The gryffon was frantically trying to reverse his momentum as the black wyrm suddenly appeared from the jungle beneath them.

The dragon's roar caused a shock wave, but Rostok deftly rose above it. The dragon flapped its wings furiously and moved its head rapidly from side to side as it searched for the enemy it could sense but not see.

Ahmad sucked in his breath as he realized why it was behaving so oddly. "Rostok, the dragon is blind."

The gryffon shook his head and roared defiantly as he dove toward the dragon. It was not Ahmad's intention to kill this dragon anymore than the last one. Once again he had no choice. He drew his sword and positioned it to inflict a fatal wound.

Ahmad could feel the heat from the dragon's fire as it shot past them, but Rostok altered his course just enough to avoid the flames. He took Ahmad directly under the dragon's belly, and the sword thrummed excitedly as Ahmad took aim.

He drove the sword home, and the dragon roared in pain. They barely cleared the dragon's underside before she suddenly dropped from the sky.

"The sword, Rostok, I must retrieve the sword."

Ahmad's mount obediently began to follow the dragon's descent. The canopy was ripped open by the wounded dragon's large girth, and the ground shook as it impacted it. The trees were still shuddering when Rostok landed. The dragon came to rest on its side, and the crystal sword was covered with green blood oozing from the wound.

Ahmad jumped from Rostok's back and rushed to the dragon. It took some effort to extricate the slick blood soaked sword from the dragon's body as if for some reason the sword was not ready to be released. Once it was free Ahmad searched the steamy jungle floor for a place to clean it. As he knelt beside a nearby pool, he studied the dragon and realized one of the toes was missing. It looked as though the dragon was still breathing.

His thoughts immediately went to Ragnar. For the first time since they were separated, he could sense Ragnar calling to him, telling him exactly where he was. Ahmad noticed Rostok was suddenly anxious, so he quickly finished cleaning the sword and stood up.

"Do you feel it too, my friend? Ragnar is near. He summons us to his side," Ahmad said, moving toward the gryffon.

Rostok did not look at him, but past him, as a low deep growl rumbled in his chest. Coming toward them was a spider unlike anything Ahmad had ever seen. It's body alone was the size of a large horse.

"You dare kill my mistress." A voice hissed in Ahmad's head.

Rostok leaped into the air and extended his claws. Before Ahmad could reach them, the spider's head was detached and the gryffon was feasting on its supple innards. Ahmad choked down the rising bile as he watched the griffon tear apart the spider.

"Rostok, we cannot delay for long. Ragnar is calling for us." He started, but Rostok was too focused on his meal to acknowledge Ahmad.

It was obvious the gryffon was not going to move until he had his fill. Ahmad cautiously climbed the rock formation and slipped past the feeding gryffon. It was the smell that led the Saracen to the opening of the dragon's lair. Ahmad heard another roar coming from somewhere deep inside.

"Peace and blessings be upon us. Have mercy on us. This is not a good omen." Ahmad muttered and glanced at Rostok. "Hurry, my friend. This is far from over."

31

Angry Thunder

by
Christian Warren Freed

Ahmad slowly picked himself off the jungle floor. The last thing he remembered was a fell voice telling him he was doomed to fail and then being knocked unconscious. He looked up as Rostok shook his head. Sensing danger, Ahmad reached for the crystal sword only to find the scabbard empty. Frowning, he searched the immediate area only to find nothing. He became frantic. The sword was his one defense against the evil hunting him. Then Rostok growled and gestured with a mighty paw. Magically or mysteriously, the sword had been cast back inside the dragon's corpse. The handle shined bright as more green blood flowed out from the wound. Great evil was at work in the jungle and it clearly intended for him to die.

Rostok tipped his massive head back and let loose a long hiss unlike anything Ahmad had heard before. His wings arched up and back. Golden feathers loosened as he stretched. The gryffon bore a wicked glare, focusing on the jungle behind Ahmad.

"What is it?" Ahmad asked gently. He turned and looked but found nothing. The jungle was quiet and unsettlingly calm—always a bad omen. Worse, he didn't have a weapon to combat any new threat. Seeing no point in continuing to stare into the near perpetual gloom of the jungle, Ahmad turned back to the dragon's corpse. He had to get that sword back. Too many lives depended on it.

He gave Rostok a final glance.

"Keep watch. Don't let anything else in."

The gryffon offered a sound that was a cross between a purr and a growl and crouched into a fighting stance as Ahmad raced back towards the dragon. Corrosive blood had already melted large patches of undergrowth making the ground unstable. Noxious fumes billowed into the air contaminating all they touched. Leaves and branches turned brown and wilted. Standing at the edge of the pollution, Ahmad desperately searched for the crystal sword unconsciously knowing it was the key to everything.

Distant branches began rustling under a lot of weight, but he couldn't worry about it now. He had to find the sword. Ahmad pulled a long strip of cloth from his pack and wrapped it around his nose and mouth to stifle a fit of coughs. Hopefully it would keep most of the fumes away.

The dragon's corpse shuddered. A dreadful hiss escaped the chest cavity. Ahmad struggled to keep his stomach from revolting. His body trembled. Every step he took felt heavy and labored. He hadn't realized until now how tired he was—how physically exhausting these last few days had been. So many thoughts collided in his head—Ragnar, the strange fair skinned Northman he'd mysteriously met in the middle of this very same jungle, the strange elemental that had befriended him when all was dark, Rostok, and Hygliak.

His mind recognized that none of this should be possible. None of the odd assortment of characters and creatures he'd encountered in this horrible land should exist. They were myths, a collection of stories dating back to the beginnings of recorded history. Yet here they were real. He walked among them, spoke to them, and bonded with them. Hygliak's death even hurt him. No one should have to suffer so. Worse, he wondered what the king and his army would think as they continued their march towards an inevitable war. Was it all connected? Was he merely a pawn in some greater cosmic game incomprehensible to the human mind? Ahmad frowned. He didn't care.

And then he spied it—the crystal sword. Miraculously it appeared undamaged! Ahmad scanned the growing pool of bright green blood hoping to find an easy path to the sword. There was none. He had no choice but to walk through the toxic blood.

"Brave little human. So eager to prove his worth," a cackling voice hissed from above.

"Yes. Watch him struggle to understand. Only he will never be able to know the truth. The land won't allow it," taunted a second.

Ahmad froze. There was no time to stop and find his assailants. He had to get the sword. Ahmad stepped into the blood. Smoke and steam rose violently as the acidity in the blood began melting Ahmad's boot. Nothing for it, he walked faster. His boots burned. Already he could feel it in the soles. He was going to melt if he didn't hurry.

More rustling distracted him. Rostok barked a twisted sound and launched into the branches. Leaves and broken branches rained down. A hairy black leg dropped heavily. Gore splashed upon contact with the soft ground. The rest of the spider's body landed right after. It had been ripped and slashed to death. Rostok dropped down behind it, spitting out a large portion of the arachnid's head.

Spider webs, thick as a man's arm, began lacing across the clearing. Soon they formed a thick canopy over Ahmad and the dragon. Dismayed, Ahmad reached down and grasped hold of the crystal sword. The weapon hummed filling him with warmth and confidence. The acid lost potency. Safe for the moment, he could at last turn his attentions to the battle at hand.

Thunder rumbled angrily across the skies. Ahmad frowned. It was a displeasure not found in Paradise, as some said. He welcomed rain, but it only served to compound matters now. He needed to get clear of these spiders and push on. The end was so very close. He felt it in his bones.

Trapped. They had no choice but to fight their way clear and beat out the approaching storm. Ahmad drew a deep breath and readied himself.

32

𝔓otions

by
Joyce Shaughnessy

Ahmad knew that he must somehow escape from the encircling spider webs. The intricately patterned nets were blocking out the sun and making it difficult to see. He heard a whimper and looked at Rostok.

Rostok had stopped feasting and was frantically trying to clean spider tissues from his feathers. His large body was being forced to bend over by the encroaching patterns. Ahmad could sense panic in his friend.

"Rostok!" Ahmad shouted sharply, "Don't fight it. Just have faith in me and the magic of this sword."

Rostok turned his frightened black eyes toward Ahmad, trying to focus on the force of his voice. He remained still as Ahmad eventually made his way through the webs and into the outside world. Rostok gladly followed him as quickly as he could.

However, what the two companions faced when they stepped out of the spider's prison was definitely more frightening!

There were ominous looking clouds everywhere they looked, but what they contained was much worse. The sound coming from them wasn't thunder but voices. The voices were muffled, and it sounded like they were talking to one another. Some of them formed vague shapes. As the two companions stepped further into the stormy land, one of the clouds suddenly shot out of the mist and said in a muted feminine voice, "We are the Maidens of Shadows. Be watchful of your surroundings, Sandman!"

Ahmad could barely make out the face of a woman! What did this mean? Was it yet another trick by the Djinn who followed them everywhere? Ahmad felt something warm in his hand, and he glanced down. *Why are the jewels glowing on this sword?* In all the time he had used it, he wondered where the special powers came from.

Just as he was pondering this new development, another cloud burst out of the darkness from the right! The mumbled voice declared, "We form what is conceived in the mind. We are the Mistresses of Storm and Earth!" Ahmad could make out another woman's face just before it disappeared into the rainclouds.

Rostok was terrified. It showed in his posture as his glossy black feathers lay against his body. His beak had all but disappeared under his stomach. His eyes were shut almost completely as he tried his best to ignore the sights and sounds around him.

Before Ahmad could think, another part of the mist rushed forward. He could make out yet another female form. "Our magic exists in ways only for which it is intended. It is beyond your understanding, o you frail human."

A familiar voice whispered behind them. "You are ours, human, because our power is infinitely stronger than yours. It is born in perpetuity!" A blue light suddenly streaked above them, and the Djinn cackled as both Ahmad and Rostok ducked to avoid it.

Ahmad turned around and said angrily, "Come out of the darkness! Face me if you believe your power stronger than mine. See how my magic sword glows? It is more powerful than your magic. Come forward, coward!"

Rostok looked at his friend with fear in his eyes. Did he know what he was doing or who he was facing?

The Djinn's voice weakened. "You will be ours in the end, Sandman, when you join the Northman. We will own both your spirits for all eternity."

As quickly as the Shadow Maidens had appeared, they were gone. The sword in Ahmad's hand stopped glowing with their passing. They vanished so quickly that Ahmad wondered if he had imagined them. What kind of world was this where such creatures existed? "Let the Magnificent one have mercy on us. Let us be gone from this land soon. We need to find Ragnar."

Ahmad again felt Ragnar summoning him, but he didn't know which way to turn. He felt there was an urgent need to find him. Selfara had mentioned that it was his fate, along with the Northman, to face the demons in this world. That time must be drawing near. His need to help Ragnar escape this world had gained another purpose. It was apparent their combined destiny was to face the beasts and to defeat them. He hoped that together they had enough power to do the deed.

***

Karlo eagerly said, "Kerr, write this down." He quickly recited the correct amounts of various potions so that they could be properly collected and written down for future reference. The two worked furiously as Ragnar waited impatiently, hoping that Karlo truly did have a potion that would neutralize the acid that the eggs were nestled in, so they could be collected.

"Ragnar, this is it! In order for you to collect the nest of dragon eggs, you must hold this flask in your hand and pour its contents into the acid pool before each step you take. Be careful to step in the correct path. Diverge from it, and you will most certainly die. We have no antidote for the acid after it has come in contact with your body."

Karlo carefully handed the container of liquid to Ragnar. He warned, "Do not spill this anywhere but on the acid in the pool. Don't even let it splash on your clothing or body. It will also burn you on contact. Be very careful!"

Ragnar stepped forward with the flask in his hands, but he did not walk as slowly as Karlo and Kerr would have liked. It made them so nervous to watch that they finally looked away praying under their breath that things would work out.

After reaching the nest, Ragnar poured the potion around the acid pool touching the eggs and then reached inside the acid puddle to retrieve them. He handled them gently so as not to break them and then put the eggs in a leather pouch, which Calyptro had produced at the last minute. He retraced his steps, carefully pouring his potion before his steps and gingerly carrying his stolen bounty. When he finally made it back on solid ground, everyone finally breathed a sigh of relief. The deed had been done.

The collective sigh of relief was temporary. Each of them knew that they had stolen very valuable property from a powerful enemy. Only Ragnar displayed the courage to destroy the dragons that were abundant in this world.

Ragnar didn't need to state that they had to leave the dead dragon's nesting place. None of them knew if another one would take over this lair. The problem now remained to decide what to do with the eggs if they hatched before the group could use them as a bargaining tool. Hopefully, that would never be necessary.

After going a short way, the travelers faced something that all of the dwellers of the ancient land horribly feared—the Cross Canyon. Ragnar didn't understand. He turned around and held out his arms, a quizzical look on his face. "Isn't it in our best interest to hurry on our journey?"

Calyptro took a step forward and put his small hand on Ragnar's powerful arm, "Ragnar, we know that a terrible fate awaits us in Cross Canyon. It is where the black lagoon exists. I have never heard of anyone who escaped it. I beg you, we must take a different course."

33

Haunted Canyon

by
H. M. Schuldt

Near a curtain of trees, Karlo looked out across the haunted canyon. He saw dark clouds increasing in the sky. A flash of lightning struck above the canyon. For a moment he wanted to see what was on the other side of the horizon. He wanted to know if it was true. Most dvergar believed that beyond the horizon was a fierce wasteland, too deadly for life. Looking at the horizon though, he thought about the secret ancient hope—a forbidden story in the Mine of Davlin. The dvergr king had tried to protect his own by teaching that only death came to those who tried to cross the canyon.

Karlo noticed reddish boulders jetting out from black water below. It looked horrific. Thunder rumbled over the dark canyon. Karlo thought about the canyon's other name to keep them out, to keep them from believing in a better world waiting for them on the other side of the canyon. "Where I come from, we call it Hell's Gate. Whoever goes in, never comes out. The king has ordered us to stay out."

"It's terrible," Calyptro shivered with fright and a troubled heart. Buried memories began to surface. "Rock trolls live in caves at the bottom. They will trample you and throw you around. Spiteful spirits will follow you and swallow you in shallow water."

"It could be a good place to get rid of the necklace if we snuck down. If Ahmad doesn't bring us the sword, we could throw the necklace in the water, and it'd be gone for all eternity," young Kerr suggested.

"No," Calyptro spoke with great fear. "If we survive the climb down, the black lagoon at the bottom has quick sand. It has thousands of corpses from battles that were fought. Even if we found a way through the black lagoon, the climb back up is impossible."

"How do you know so much about this place?" Karlo asked, feeling hot and thirsty.

"I know someone who died in the canyon. He thought it was the way out." Calyptro reluctantly spoke. His voice began to soften. He felt guilty. Painful memories pressed in his mind. He had once tried to stop his brother from crossing, but he failed. "We must find a different way. There is nothing but death in the canyon."

Ragnar looked around and saw rock cliffs extending for miles on both sides. He felt Ahmad was somewhere close by, and Ragnar knew he would see his desert friend again. Ragnar paid no attention to Calyptro's sorrow. "Tell me, lizard man, how can I reach the other side?"

"Do you seek your own doom?" Calyptro asked, his voice still weak. "Haven't you heard what I said? This is the most advanced rock climbing I've ever seen. Sir, there is no way we will make it down."

"You see this axe in my hand?" Ragnar said. Lightning struck again. "I'm going to hack off your lizard head unless you tell me how to get to the other side."

"Enough! No more threats!" Karlo said. Somewhere near loud thunder boomed.

"Be that as it may, I'm dead already in this place." Calyptro could hardly sense Ragnar's stubbornness in the midst of his own painful memories. "I have no idea how to get across. My brother died down there. He thought he could get through it. He never returned."

Karlo called for silence when he held up his hand. "Maybe he made it to the other side. If not, may he rest in peace."

"We are not doomed to die, lizard man," Ragnar said. "I've seen this place before. It was a vision from the halls of Valhalla. It is my duty to go across." He was about to describe the vision of a big dragonfly and *something in a tree* when Karlo gave a suggestion.

"Calyptro," Karlo said. "Do you know a good hiding spot close by where we can hide the dragon eggs near acid water?"

"I know this place like the back of my hand," Calyptro replied.

"There is a plan that we can agree on," Karlo said.

Ragnar took four eggs out of the leather pouch. Light turquoise with black specks, they felt as hard as a rock. One of these dragon eggs was bigger than the other three. Karlo placed the three smaller eggs in separate cloth bags. Ragnar kept the bigger one, preparing for the next conflict.

"Master, why does the big one have red streaks on it?" Kerr asked.

"I don't know why it is different. It's just a matter of time before the parent of these eggs comes back," Karlo said nervously.

"Ahmad and the crystal sword are close by. I will stay here on the edge of this cliff and stare down into Hell's Gate," Ragnar spoke with confidence. "Go. Make your way to hide the rest of the eggs. Don't place them in the acid! Watch out for spiders! And watch out for spider webs!"

Within seconds Karlo and Calyptro were off to a secret hiding place with all but one of the dragon eggs.

"Some of the webs are as strong as steel," the young dvergr said.

Kerr and the beetle stood watch to keep Ragnar safe. The beetle moved along the surface of the Earth in short bursts of energy as if he were searching for a lookout post.

"What did you say about spider webs?" Ragnar asked, remembering that someone said this earlier in his dragonfly vision.

As Kerr spoke, his words carried an echo in the wind. "Some… webs… are as strong… as steel."

"That's it!" Ragnar surrounded himself in these words.

"What?" Kerr asked.

"In my dragonfly vision, something was in a tree when I heard those words." Ragnar sought to understand but came up empty. He was eager to figure out the meaning of the vision, marveled that he had recognized the familiar words. He knew Odin would reveal more pieces from the great feasting hall of Valhalla.

Ragnar sat in a warm breeze. He held the big speckled egg turning it around and around. It would die soon without the acid solution. He thought about the vicious creature inside and almost smashed it right then. He would have struck all of the eggs, but he kept his word to use them if they needed to. The red streaks were unusually irregular. Looking closely on the egg, he found a dark script. It read,

Levethix

He saw that word recently on a journal he confiscated from the dragon's lair. Retrieving the journal from his leather pouch, he read,

Darustrix Irthos: Levethix

"Blessed Odin, what do these words mean? Please show me." Ragnar sent his prayer to Asgard, a land in the sky.

34

Master Climber

by
Randall Lemon

As Ragnar spoke his prayer to All-Father Odin, he raised his eyes skyward as if seeking an entrance to the Bifrost Bridge or perhaps Heimdall, its guardian. Instead, his eyes were greeted by something quite unexpected. As his eyes sought the heavens, they were blocked by the silhouette of a huge tree that rose from the nearby edge of the haunted Cross Canyon. Ragnar's vigilant gaze noted something quite odd high up near the crown of the tree. From where he stood it was but a shadow, and somehow seemed to be a familiar one.

Ragnar turned to his remaining companions. "Which one of you is up for a small climb?" he asked.

Of course, it was Kerr who volunteered immediately. "Show me the wall you wish me to scale, friend Ragnar, and I will be at the top before you can say my uncle's name three times."

Ragnar took the young dvergr by his shoulders and turned him to face away from the walls of the canyon and pointed him in the direction of the huge tree. "There is the cliff I wish you to climb. High up in its branches, I see something that does not belong there. It is almost at the very top of the tree. Go there and bring it back to me and anything else you may find that strikes you as unusual."

"Eek ffft uh, that's a tree—not a wall. I've been trained to climb walls from the time I took my first steps," Kerr stammered. "I have never climbed a tree. What could possibly be of use up there? No, climbing a tree would be a silly thing to do!"

Ragnar appraised the dvergr and pressed on, "Well, I guess every man fears something, and I can see that this tree must be what you fear. Just the thought of climbing it is bringing a green tinge to your face and a yellow one to your back. Mayhaps I can find someone whose courage has not fled at the sight of his leafy opponent."

"I'm not afraid," retorted Kerr. "I've got as much courage as anyone here, even you Ragnar. And I will prove it." With that the dvergr moved tentatively to the tree and began his ascent.

As Ragnar watched Kerr climbing, he could not hide the smile on his face. He had known that Kerr was the best choice for this particular mission and just needed the proper motivation. As the dvergr moved from handhold to handhold and branch to branch, Ragnar felt like a proud father. He began to realize, with some shock, just how close he had grown to his small companions over a relatively short time.

Before he came to this strange land, Ragnar would have never given any thought to dvergar and goblins and the other lesser races, as some men termed them, in regards to traits like courage, honor, and nobility. But since he had come here, he had seen those traits exhibited time and again by his smaller seemingly insignificant companions.

Perhaps this is one reason I have been sent on this adventure, to realize that all beings have worth, Ragnar thought. *In truth, it is not just men and gods who show they are deserving of respect. By Odin, I could not have come this far without their help. I swear that in the future, I will not measure a man in inches. Rather I will measure all creatures by the length and breadth of their spirit.*

A shout broke into Ragnar's reverie, "Ragnar! I can see it. It looks to be a heavy crossbow with a quarrel strapped to it. It has bolts for the bow. I will try to reach it. It looks too heavy for me to carry down."

Ragnar cupped his hands and shouted upward. "Just see if you can dislodge it and let it fall down. It will get snagged on its way down. You can continue the process until it falls free, and I can catch it down here."

And that is precisely what Kerr did. Gradually the bow made its way down the length of the tree. Kerr had thought it wise to strap the case of bolts to his own belt. Once Ragnar had caught the mighty crossbow, the young dvergr scampered down the bough of the tree and ran up to Ragnar beaming with joy.

"See Ragnar! I told you, I ain't afraid of nothing."

Ragnar patted Kerr affectionately on the head, "Yes Kerr, it appears true that you have the heart of a brave warrior. Let none ever claim otherwise in my presence."

"Look how odd these crossbow bolts are," Kerr said. "They appear both longer and fatter than usual bolts and they appear to be made of some odd material."

Ragnar inspected one of the bolts, which Kerr handed to him. "By Hel and the gods of Asgard, I believe you are correct. These bolts feel more like they are made of some tightly compacted material than of wood."

"Let us load and fire one and see what happens."

With that Ragnar loaded the crossbow and fired at a tree some distance from where they stood. The bolt sprang from the bow. Trailing behind was a fine silk cord. The further the bolt went, more line played out and the smaller the bolt became. Finally it *thunked* into the chosen tree.

Ragnar tested the line and was surprised by the strength of the silk rope. A plan began to form in his barbarian mind.

By now, all the companions had returned. Ragnar faced them, "Not only has Kerr suggested a solution to our problem in crossing the dreaded swamp and avoiding the spiteful spirits that inhabit this canyon, he has provided us with the means of effecting his solution. You are a pearl of great price, Kerr."

Kerr was completely mystified by the praises heaped on him by Ragnar, but they all soon learned what he meant.

"All the dangers of this canyon appear to spring from the bottom, so we will just avoid walking across the bottom." Ragnar began using his champion axe to cut through the tough material of the line that stretched from the bow to the tree. He made six short segments. When he was done, he fired a second bolt higher up into the bole of the tree.

"Now all we need to do is climb up there and practice will begin."

Calyptro finally spoke up. "What kind of practice?"

Ragnar smiled broadly and began stalking off to the tree. "*Slide practice.*"

After some hours had passed, everyone finally got the hang of it. Then they climbed to the highest point on their side of the canyon. Ragnar picked out a target tree somewhat lower than their current position and fired the bow setting a line over the top of the canyon.

"Just like Kerr said," Ragnar stated. "Webs as strong as steel. Now we will slide our way across this haunted ravine far above the dangers that lurk below."

And with that, the barbarian wrapped his segment of line over the rope and began his slide over Cross Canyon.

35

Writing On the Wall

by
Lynette White

Rostok returned to the air. Once they were free of the ground, Ahmad's mind calmed. He instinctively knew where he would find Ragnar. They were flying toward the sun when a movement in the air caught Ahmad's attention.

He squinted his eyes to discern his next foe, but Rostok's keen eyes already knew who was approaching, and so Rostok whistled. The Saracen was surprised by the sound he had never heard before. It almost sounded happy.

Rostok flapped his great wings and pushed forward. A similar whistle echoed across the sky in response. Ahmad sucked in his breath when more followed. He counted eight distinctive calls.

"Mighty and Majestic is He; gryffons," he gasped.

As they dropped below the sun's glare, Ahmad could make out the tight formation. Movement on the ground drew Ahmad's attention away from the approaching gryffons. On the plain below him was the steady movement of an army. Walking among them were several goblins. Hygliak's sacrifice stirred Ahmad's mind.

"Ahmad!" A voice called across the sky.

Ahmad smiled at Simurgh's voice. He was leading the others toward him. Ahmad pointed toward the ground, and Simurgh nodded. They landed a short distance away from the main camp.

Ahmad and Simurgh slid from their gryffons simultaneously and hurried toward each other. They wrapped their arms loosely around each other's shoulders.

"Ahmad, my friend, it is good to see you again." Simurgh greeted him and stepped back. "I see Rostok is still taking good care of you."

"It is good to see you again as well, Simurgh. I am surprised to see you back in the air. What are you doing here?"

Simurgh laughed. "As I told you when we parted, my friend, I have many mounts." He gently stroked Rostok on the neck. "Rostok here is one of my favorites. We are in the King's service. Today we are looking for a frost giant who attacked our forward flank two days ago. He killed several brave soldiers and disappeared like the cowards they are." He explained and dropped his hand.

"How is your journey? Have you found your friend?"

Ahmad smiled ruefully. "It has been a journey unlike any I could have ever imagined in my worse nightmares, but thanks to Rostok, we have overcome every obstacle placed before us. I am on my way to Ragnar now. I feel him summoning me, and I know he is near."

Simurgh nodded knowingly. "So this Ragnar is the one who uses the summoning stone." His hand spanned the riders behind him. "We have all felt its call after generations of silence, but we did not know whom we seek. The king wishes to offer his assistance to the legendary Gryffon Master. It is indeed fortunate that we meet again, but I am not surprised."

"I will not delay you any longer. But will you relay the king's message to Ragnar?"

For the first time since waking up in this dreadful place, Ahmad felt hope, and he smiled. "I will, Simurgh, but before I go I wish to convey a tale of great bravery to the goblins."

* * *

The party gathered up on the opposite side of the canyon. Poor Jesper was so horrified he screamed clear across the canyon, and Kerr nearly lost his grip because he was more concerned about the scarab in his pocket than his own safety. Karlo, Kerr, Calyptro, and Ragnar left the still trembling Jesper under Barry's care to tend to more pressing matters.

"Now where do we go?" Ragnar asked. "Karlo, any ideas?"

The dvergr shook his head and shrugged. "Do not look at me, my friend. I have no idea if a dvergr has ever been on this side of the canyon."

All eyes went to the scarab at Kerr's feet, but it was Calyptro who slowly stirred and turned toward a tall cliff nearby.

"The dvergr tunnels," Calyptro muttered.

"The what?" Ragnar and Karlo asked in unison.

The odd lizard pointed toward the cliff. "I believe the dvergar have been here before. There is a legend told of the dvergr tunnels where there was a horrible battle between good and evil. If my memory serves me correctly, they should be right over there."

"Take us there, lizard man," Ragnar demanded.

Calyptro nodded and started to lead the way. Before long they came upon a man-made opening in the cliff wall untouched for eons of time. Everyone felt a chill as they stopped—not even a cobweb violated this place.

Calyptro looked at Ragnar with a plea in his eyes to reconsider. To his dismay Ragnar drew his axe and pointed toward the doorway. The absolute silence inside the tunnel was unnerving and filled with strange anticipation. It was an eternal reverence, almost seeming to request worship and awe.

Calyptro led them through the small tunnel until it opened up into a large natural cavern. Karlo held his torch up and pointed toward a far wall covered in writing.

"Blessed Odin," Ragnar whispered. "Can you read that Karlo?"

"Yes I can. It is written in an older form of our native tongue, but I can decipher it easily enough. He moved toward the wall and started to read it, but then he paused.

I leave this so the truth is known.

Ragnar urged him to continue, so Karlo cleared his throat and adjusted his torch.

Our tale starts when a young apprentice was taken by Traven the Fallen and forced to make a necklace for his beloved Thora. He had the stones placed in an exact pattern. Then Traven used his powers to imbue the gems with unspeakable evil.

To prove his love to Thora, his final touch was to place a part of his own soul in the largest gem before presenting it to her.

Traven had all the powers of the Light Elementals until he was banished for committing an unspeakable crime. With his beloved Thora at his side, Traven was determined to rule this land and no one was spared from his and Thora's evil wrath.

To stop Traven's reign of terror, the Light Elementals crafted a crystal sword and a summoning stone. They called upon their warrior allies, the Gryffon Riders, and entrusted them with the quest to stop Traven and Thora. Among the riders were two strangers from far away lands. To the dark-skinned stranger was given the sword as he was the purest in heart. The summoning stone was given to the other as he lead the mighty Gryffon Riders.

I could no longer bear to stand as a witness to the evil being done by the necklace I was forced to create. As Thora and Traven slept, I stole the necklace and fled.

While Traven gathered his army to get revenge for my betrayal, the dvergar gathered to stand against him. The Gryffon Riders arrived with the sword to destroy the necklace, and we should have done so the moment they arrived. Instead we shared stories while Traven prepared his attack. His forces were upon us in an instant and his wrath was fierce.

I offered to sacrifice myself to protect our people, but the king refused my wish, declaring the dvergar will make a stand. Instead, I was told to seek refuge deep in the caverns to keep the necklace away from Traven and Thora. The battle raged for hours and, when it finally fell silent, I returned to destroy the necklace. I found the dark-skinned warrior among the dead and not far from Traven's body.

I frantically searched for the crystal sword, but learned from the survivors that Thora had killed the dark-skinned warrior and ripped the sword from his hand after he had killed her beloved Traven. She fled with what was left of their forces and took the crystal sword with her. We have tended to the dead the best we could, and now a few survivors and I will travel with the Gryffon Master on a quest to find the crystal sword and destroy the evil I was forced to create.

- Karagon, Dvergr Tribe of Valinn

Karlo fell silent, and Ragnar stared at the wall as everything suddenly made perfect sense—the sword, the tomb, the necklace, the summoning stone, and even Karlo's words about their destiny. But the stark reality was that he might never return home, and it weighed heavy on his heart.

"Tribe of Valinn?" Kerr whispered. "That means we are his."

Karlo's eyes were on Ragnar. "Aye lad, it does."

Karlo's hand went to the pocket where he kept the necklace. Everything had come full circle now. The only thing missing was the crystal sword.

Ragnar started to walk out of the tunnel, and the others silently followed. They stepped outside when a dark shadow crossed over in the sky. The Viking instinctively reached for his axe. He was immediately alert when he looked up, sucking in his breath. Flying above him was a gryffon, and looking down at him was the one face that brought him to tears.

"Ragnar, our Master! Peace be upon you," Ahmad shouted as Rostok came in for a landing.

36

A Kingly Gift

by
Christian Warren Freed

"I had thought you dead," the Northman said with exuberance. He hadn't exactly bonded with Ahmad in the short period of time they'd been together and held certain levels of resentment for being left alone in the jungle to fight the frost giant. Still, Ahmad looked nothing like he had only days ago. Whatever trials he had faced were certainly equal to Ragnar's own.

Ahmad bowed curtly. "Death has come for me many times in many guises. It appears I am meant for other things though, according to my destiny."

Ragnar regarded his companion. "It also appears you have quite a tale for the telling."

"Indeed, but it is long and harrowing. I shall not bore you with how I came to be here, but I feel compelled to explain my last adventure, for it is dire and holds ill portent to both of our futures." Ahmad exhaled deeply and began his recounting. His last sights were of a large group of spiders trailing after him.

Rostok dropped into a defensive posture and wheeled around to face the jungle. Trees swayed heavily without any winds. Branches cracked and broke. Storming after them with unabated fury and hatred, evil was on its way. The gryffon squawked, flaring his wings. Taking a deep inhale and then steadying his breath, Ahmad slowly turned. Slender legs poked into the sunlight.

Ahmad dearly wanted to go home. He'd been through too much in such a short period of time. It was not a life he was meant to live. Thoughts of returning to Damascus and his desert home were little more than a fanciful distraction. This was reality. Here. Now. He gripped his sword tighter and readied for whatever new horror this world seemed determined to throw at him.

"Will these accursed things never tire?" he asked the skies. Ahmad cursed. He didn't know why, but unspoken urges whispered for him to mount the gryffon and flee. The spiders hadn't given up.

Ragnar rubbed the stubble on his chin. "You say they are hunting you even now?"

Ahmad nodded. "They are moving at speed. Even my impromptu meeting with Simurgh was not enough to shake them. I fear they will be here shortly."

"That is dire news indeed, for I have much to do if we are to ever stop the evil polluting this land and return to our homes," Ragnar admitted.

Ahmad clasped his hands behind his back and began to pace. Try as he might, he couldn't come to any plausible conclusion without them separating again. Too many along the way had hinted at the importance of Ragnar's quest. Ahmad must relent and give the Northman time to finish his task, even if it meant sacrificing himself in the process.

"Perhaps I have a solution," the man from Damascus said. "I will take Rostok and lead the spiders away, giving you enough time to end this evil."

"Alone? That would be suicide," Ragnar replied tersely.

Ahmad smiled. "You are not alone. You have your collection of companions, and I have met many along my path as well. There is an army out there, moving fast and in great strength. Their king has come to do battle with the great enemy and aid us as necessary."

"That is most welcome news mixed with risky proposition," the Northman agreed. "I would give you a token to help your fight. It is a staff made from the World Tree. My people have long revered Yggdrasil and its powers. It will help you defeat the spiders."

Ahmad accepted the slender shaft of polished wood. "A kingly gift. My thanks, Northman."

"Use it well. I fear that anything less will only result in our demise. How far away is this army?"

"Less than a day's march from here," Ahmad replied. "I fear they do not know your location though."

Ragnar's eyebrow rose questioningly. "It appears you have the means of solving that problem."

Rostok flared his wings and roared.

"Indeed. Very well. I shall fly Rostok back to the army and lead them here. Perhaps together the king and I can remove the spider threat, for I feel they are part of the greater problem. There is more…"

"More? I am not so sure my heart can handle more," Ragnar said.

The Saracen grinned. "No, my friend. This is a most welcome boon." He withdrew the crystal sword and handed it hilt first to Ragnar. "This was always meant to be yours during the final battle."

Ragnar accepted the blade, which he had only glimpsed for a moment at the beginning of their adventures. His eyes were drawn to the blade, the way the hilt fit comfortably in his palm as if crafted specifically for him. "I think we might be able to win after all. Fare thee well, Ahmad."

They clasped forearms. "You as well, Ragnar. May we meet again in better times." Reluctantly he climbed aboard the great creature and lifted off to fight horrific spiders in the jungle.

37

A Soldier's Arrow

by

Joyce Shaughnessy

Woldar knew that he was dying.

He heard the frost giant's mighty roar before the terrible creature was upon him. Woldar had no way to escape the beast and no means to fight him. With one swipe of his mighty paw, the giant threw his body across the ground like a piece of rubbish and destroyed the only home Woldar had known while living in this strange world. The giant left him with nothing, not even his friend Kylo for comfort.

Woldar's last thought before dying, *My greatest regret is that even if Ragnar is able to keep his promise to come for me, it will be too late. I know that I will never see my beloved England again.*

***

Ahmad soon encountered the nest of spiders and valiantly fought them with the wooden staff given to him by Ragnar. It wasn't easy at first, but he found enough power within the staff, and he was able to fight off the arachnids. He quickly dispatched each of the spiders by cutting them into pieces.

In order to make certain the spiders were dead, Rostok picked up the pieces and spit out their offensive remains. A grateful look from Ahmad was enough to earn his eternal loyalty. Never had a gryffon shown a sandman this much kindness.

Ragnar had been correct. The spiders were defenseless against the staff made from the mighty Yggdrasil tree. Ahmad gasped in relief when he was free of them. Ahmad smiled ruefully because he knew that this battle with them would not be his last before returning to his homeland.

After destroying the arachnids, Ahmad mounted Rostok again and went in search of Simurgh and his king's army. There was no doubt in his mind that they would be needed at the final battle.

As Ahmad came upon the army's campsite, he felt grateful that he had met Simurgh. He landed and told him of his exploits with the spiders.

Simurgh said, "I am relieved to see you well after doing battle with such dangerous enemies. But we must not linger. We heard the mighty roar of a frost giant and felt his chilling breath in the distance. I'm sorry we can't give you and Rostok time to rest, but I am afraid we must hurry in order to escape his rage. We can't afford to lose any of our soldiers before reaching your friend, Ragnar."

"I agree. Let's take to the sky again."

It wasn't long before Simurgh and Ahmad heard the roar of the frost giant and felt the great chill of his breath. Rostok was immediately at attention with his sleek dark feathers flat against his body, and his nose flared in anticipation.

Simurgh and Ahmad quickly looked at each other and nodded in agreement as they dove for the ground, ready to make a stand before the monster they had hoped to evade.

When they landed, the ground shook from the giant's heavy steps. Soldiers stood at attention beside their gryffons with their bows and arrows drawn to fight.

As the enormous frost giant appeared before them, Ahmad held up the staff and prayed, "In the name of the all Merciful, the all Compassionate, I seek protection from this cursed evil. Please aid us in destroying this terrible creature so that we may continue on our quest."

Just before the creature could reach them and as Simurgh nodded his head, the soldiers skillfully launched arrows in the air, aiming for his heart. The monstrous giant fell to his death, but only after emitting one last agonizing roar.

Amazingly, they hadn't lost a single soldier or gryffon. They were about to mount their gryffons when Simurgh pointed and said, "Look. There's someone on the ground under that tree."

Ahmad was amazed when he inspected the dead man. "It's another human! I have always been under the assumption that Ragnar and I were the only humans in this world. I wonder where he came from and how he got here. The frost giant must have killed him. I wonder if Ragnar knew he was here. What a terrible thing it must be to die alone."

Ahmad and Simurgh agreed that it was only proper to bury the man. After they had completed the task, Ahmad closed his eyes and whispered a prayer of mourning for him.

Ahmad ended his prayer with, "Knock, and He'll open the door. Vanish, and He'll make you shine like the sun. Fall, and He'll raise you to the heavens. Become nothing, and He'll turn you into everything. Have mercy on him. Please accept this prayer."

Out of the darkness came an answer, one that filled Ahmad with dread. "There will be no mercy for you or the light-skinned man. Your soul will spend eternity serving me."

Ahmad thought, *Why is the boneman always near? He even haunts me in my prayers.* He announced, "It is time for us to leave this place of death."

Night had begun to fall, but the group hurried on. Ahmad could feel his way even in the dark. Something was pulling him back toward Ragnar. It was his final destiny. Fate was sending him, no matter what the outcome.

38

Darustrix Irthos

by
H. M. Schuldt

Ragnar held onto the crystal sword. Powerful lightning bolts struck invading the night jungle. "And now the moment has arrived! Karlo, place the necklace across this fallen tree and hold the ends."

Karlo reached into his pocket. A frightening boom hit, followed by a terrible gust of westerly wind. The breeze felt warm like a hiss of wind only a gold dragon could make.

Calyptro turned his green lizard head toward the trees and saw the wind grow strong. A ghastly rotting smell came rushing toward him. He spotted a group of croaking amphibian men hopping rapidly from upwind. The one who led the way had a severe hump back, and he was wearing a hard helmet. The creatures had webbed toes and thick leathery skin covered in warts. They wore short green trousers and had a flimsy helmet. These were not wicked folk. If they have a fault, it is the way they could aimlessly squirt venomous toxin when attacked.

The amphibian leader flicked his tongue and called out in a gruff voice. "Anthropoid, what is a black dragon doing on this side of the canyon?"

"Anthropoid? This is my human friend, Ragnar," Calyptro called out into the wind. "He has come to fight evil spirits that plague our world. Where is this black dragon you speak of? And who are you?"

"I am Wesley, the leader of the Marine Toads. A black dragon landed in our home. It's Barrel the Terrible. He's in a fit of rage because someone killed his mate and stole his eggs. One of his eggs is a wizard dragon with red marks. If you find it, you have to smash it. It's the dragon's secret, you know, Darustrix Irthos—it means *dragon secret*. The dragon egg with the red streaks is a Levethix—it means *wizard*. We were forced to leave everything behind in our home at Leafy Park." The amphibian leader motioned for his group to continue on to the haunted canyon. "We are on our way down to the Black Lagoon. Sandy soil down there, nice and wet. We go at once!"

"My helmet! You found my helmet!" Ragnar called out. Hopping by in single file were several amphibian men who had muscular hind legs.

"This is your helmet?" Wesley asked. "Do you want it back?"

"I lost it when I was transported here," Ragnar answered. "May I have it back?"

Wesley pulled hard, and the helmet let out a loud suction noise. He tossed it to Ragnar.

"Where can we find Leafy Park?" Ragnar asked. He positioned his helmet, and it was good to feel whole again.

Wesley called out. "On the other side of the great Redwoods. You can find shelter in the Redwoods, but we will take shelter in the Black Lagoon. A storm is coming!"

The croaking men and their toad stench disappeared into the jungle. As fast as the sudden wind began, it suddenly stopped. Misty air became thick, protecting them in seclusion.

Karlo pulled the necklace out of his pocket. He knelt down and placed it on a fallen tree. Time seemed to slow down as the group huddled around. Ragnar prepared the crystal sword above his head.

"For the home of Calyptro is worth more than all the treasure on Earth," Ragnar said, "and to me, it is where I discovered new friends. You shall have your jungle back, lizard man, without the Lich King. Calyptro, prepare the false stone. Be quick to replace the evil stone, the large ruby in the middle."

Ragnar raised the sword with two arms as if to pierce the center stone. Lightning flashed again. A chilling cry of banshees called out from the jungle. They heard a cry of liches as they fought Simurgh's army. Thunder boomed, and the sword became radiant.

The crystal sword came slowly toward the center stone. As if a magnet opposed the destruction, Ragnar pushed down with all his might. He pushed closer toward the large red stone. Sparks flew out in all directions. It bothered Barry's beady eyes, and he had to turn away. Everyone had to squint or turn away except for Calyptro and his bright glowing eyes.

Finally the sword touched down. A brilliant flash shot straight up toward the halls of Valhalla. Calyptro saw the glowing red stone begin to dull.

Ragnar held onto the sword with all his strength. Waves of energy flowed out from Traven's crafted weapon. The red stone soon faded and turned foggy black. Four prongs surrounding the evil ruby opened up. All this confirmed why he had to cross the canyon.

A choir of screams called out from deep in the jungle. It was done. Prophecy had been fulfilled. Traven the Lich King was completely dead. He was ushered into the eternal prison in the city of the dead for his terrible crimes.

"It is finished." Kerr spoke first.

"Not quite." Karlo knew better. He let go of the necklace and stood up. "Replace the stone, Calyptro."

The lizard man quickly knelt down and pulled the black stone out of the necklace with his green fingers. He handed the black stone to Ragnar. The light-skinned human looked at the powerless stone closely and saw his own reflection on one side. Calyptro fastened the false gem into position. It looked as good as new for one more day. The false gem would eventually fade when Horgoth's spell ended.

"A mighty gift for a gold dragon if we should happen to stumble upon one," young Kerr said.

Karlo placed the necklace back in his pocket to get rid of it as ordered by his king, Andren, from the Dwarf Mine of Davlin.

They marched through the Redwoods closer to Leafy Park. Calyptro spoke quietly to Ragnar. "I was down on myself for not saving my brother from going into the canyon. And I was down on myself for not saving Woldar from Jungle Fever. I'm not worth much. But now that I helped replace Traven's stone, I'm beginning to feel better. You saved my home. You saved this place from the Lich King and his minions. I owe you my life and I am forever grateful."

All the company of Valhalla watched as Ragnar stopped in the middle of the thick Redwoods.

"All things have worth, my lizard friend." Ragnar spoke his learned lesson. "It's dark. We need a good night's sleep. This is a tight spot in the Redwoods. We'll settle here. It's a good place to rest. In the morning we will eat, defeat Barrel, and crush the egg."

"We might need it as a bargaining tool, Ragnar," Karlo reminded.

Kerr called out on his piccolo three times using a familiar melody. Within minutes, an owl soared into the Redwoods and landed close to Kerr and the beetle. This friendly owl watched over them for several hours giving them comfort.

Ragnar and his jungle friends slept still with both eyes shut.

* * *

Barrel the Terrible tossed and turned in a fit of rage. Leaves flew out in every direction. He frequently opened one eye throughout the night in his moist leafy nest. He would take any hostage to find out what happened to his prized eggs. At dawn, the angry dragon entered the Redwoods. The owl gave an alarming hoot, not loud enough, and he flew to safety. Soon Barrel found the sleeping travelers. The terrible dragon gave Kerr a sleeping poison, and he quietly took the young dvergr back to his den.

39

𝕭arrel's 𝕯en

by
Randall Lemon

Early the next morning, the shrill screaming of Karlo awakened Ragnar. The Northman had celebrated the destruction of both the enchanted stone and his enemies, the lich and frost giants, by imbibing a fair amount of *jungle juice* supplied by Barry last night.

Ragnar opened one bloodshot eye and growled at Karlo. "Pipe down, and let a man enjoy a well-deserved rest!"

Ragnar tried to reclose that red orb, but Karlo would have none of it. "Wake up, you slumbering lummox!" He followed his exclamation with a swift kick to the ample buttocks of the Northman.

Ragnar jumped to his feet rubbing the injured part of his anatomy. Had he not shared so many adventures with the old dvergr, he would have been tempted to reshape the top of his skull with the flat of his champion ax. But he could see now through the red haze of two partly opened eyes that Karlo was really upset about something. "Okay, what new disaster has befallen us while I tried to get a little sleep?"

Karlo pointed to a pile of rags next to the now-cold

campfire. "Kerr has disappeared! He was taken in the night from beneath our very noses."

Ragnar stopped rubbing his aching rump and started rubbing his aching head. Barry's jungle juice had quite a kick to it. "Is that all? He's probably just gone off into the trees to make water. Something I myself am going to need to do soon."

Karlo hopped over and grabbed the pile of rags and shoved them under Ragnar's bulbous nose. "Then explain this!"

Ragnar looked wearily at the rags and wrinkled his nose at the odor. "It's just a pile of foul-smelling rags, so what?"

Karlo smiled triumphantly, "Sure, that's what it is now! But these used to be Kerr's beautiful cloak and warm sleeping blanket. Now they are riddled with ugly holes. And if you would just gather your wits, you would recognize that odor for what it is: *Acid!*"

Ragnar tried to shake the cobwebs from his head and clear his blurry vision. "So what is your point? Where did your young nephew wander off to?"

"Kerr didn't wander off anywhere, and that is precisely my point," Karlo stated excitedly. "The ground here is soft and yet there are no tracks going away from where Kerr slept. He did not wander off anywhere. He was taken by something that could fly, so it left no prints on the ground. It's something that drips acid from its giant maw. Am I being clear enough to you now?"

Light dawned slowly within the craggy skull of the barbarian warrior. "A black dragon, Barrel. He must have come in the night and taken your apprentice, but why? What does he hope to gain?"

Seeing that Ragnar was finally clear-headed enough to understand, Karlo grasped Ragnar by his two shoulders and stared closely into his eyes, "It could be... Barrel has found out that we took the eggs and hid them. No doubt he will try to force Kerr into telling him their location. Since we split the eggs up and hid them separately, Kerr won't be able to reveal the location of any eggs other than the one he hid. If Barrel doesn't immediately kill Kerr in a fit of rage, he might try to use him to trade with us for all the eggs. We must hurry to the Black Lagoon and ask the Marine Toads what they know about the *dragon secret: wizard*. Then we must go to the edge of Cross Canyon and get the eggs and offer to trade them with Barrel for Kerr's life."

Calyptro and Barry had been holding a whispered conversation on the side. Finally Barry nodded, and Calyptro stepped forward. "Karlo, I am sorry, we have all grown to love your young nephew. But that is precisely what we cannot do. You heard what Wesley said last night. We cannot allow Barrel to regain the red-striped egg. If the egg hatches, think of all the mischief that a Dragon Wizard could unleash on our world. Do you believe, for even a second, that Kerr would want to be responsible for the death and destruction that would follow? To that end, Barry and I have resolved to not reveal the location of the eggs we hid away, not even to you, my friend." As he spoke these words, Calyptro's throat tightened and tears appeared in his eyes.

Karlo released Ragnar's shoulders and ran to Calyptro throwing himself down in front of him. "Do you understand that you are pronouncing a death sentence on my nephew through your stubbornness? You must relent and tell us where the eggs are, or Kerr is doomed, and his death will be on your conscience."

More tears poured from Calyptro's eyes. "So be it, for I can more easily bear his one death on my conscience that the death of hundreds, maybe thousands, that would result from the hatching of that red-striped egg and the other black dragon eggs.

Now Barry spoke up, "We will do everything we can to help save Kerr from the evil black dragon. We will risk our own lives, but we will not give back the eggs."

* * *

While the companions tried to find a mutually agreeable way to save their friend from Barrel, Kerr was lying unconscious in the dirt in front of Barrel's lair. Above him attached to the wall were some corroded metal straps, which had once held Kerr's right arm pinioned in them. Barrel had tried frightening the intrepid little dvergr into revealing what had happened to the eggs. But Kerr had refused to give any information at all. Seeing that his threats were useless, Barrel had some of his minions imprison Kerr standing with his arm outstretched away from the rest of his body.

Barrel asked again, and when Kerr stood mute, the mighty dragon raised his salivating jaws above the arms and allowed a small amount of his acid to drip down onto the dvergr's arm. Immediately where the drops fell on Kerr's arm, the flesh hissed and burnt. Terrible blistering sores opened up. Then Barrel asked again, but Kerr clenched his teeth and refused to give the dragon any satisfaction. So Barrel continued letting drop after drop sear into the dvergr's flesh. Finally brave little Kerr could keep quiet no longer and gave forth with an agonizing scream. By now most of the flesh on his arm had burned away. Raw sinew and even bits of white bone were clearly visible where the dragon's acid had exposed them.

Kerr was practically driven insane by the pain and finally revealed that he knew only the hiding place of one egg which he readily revealed. Barrel refused to believe him and kept drooling onto Kerr's arm until the appendage was completely eaten through. Kerr no longer was held up by the arm, which the dragon had deprived him of.

Now Kerr's screams were silenced, and there was a terrible stillness in the air while Barrel contemplated his next move. The dragon was tempted to just swallow what was left of his prisoner whole. But that would bring the dragon no closer to the other missing eggs. He sent his minions to recover the one egg at the locale Kerr had indicated and to search the surrounding area in hopes of finding the others—especially his most precious red-striped egg. If Barrel ate the youth, he might never manage to get the others to reveal the location of the wizard egg.

"Perhapsss I can ssseek them out and offer to trade thissss onesss life for my eggsssss," reasoned Barrel.

Unfortunately for the evil reptile, unbeknownst to him events had already moved beyond that point. Barrel had sent all his minions to search not knowing that, even while suffering excruciating pain, Kerr had not revealed the real location of the missing eggs. Now those minions were headed in the totally wrong direction to search, and Barrel was on his own—unprotected.

Karlo, Ragnar, and the others had spoken to the Marine Toads. They had been so eager to see an end to the hideous monster that they sent along scouts to lead the friends to the dragons lair. The small party was closing in on Barrel's lair even now.

Their plan was simplicity itself. The Marine Toads, Calyptro, and Barry would allow Ragnar and Karlo to precede them to the jungle's edge near Barrel's den. Then the rest would approach making noise to attract the dragon's attention. It would be risky for them as, instead of investigating, the dragon might just unleash its deadly breath weapon on the area of their approach. If Barrel moved forth to investigate the source of the noise, Karlo would use his short bow on a chosen mark, one of the dragon's large luminous eyes. If his aim was true, the small arrow would penetrate with enough force for the dragon to draw back his head in pain, and then Ragnar would seize upon that moment to rush forth with his champion axe to take the dragon's toe and then end its life. And this time there would be no mistake and no redemption for the evil reptile. Ragnar meant to deprive Barrel of his head as well.

The plan almost worked to perfection. Unfortunately while the dragon did move forward to investigate, he still chose to unleash a deadly breath. All that saved Calyptro and the others from certain death was that they were still slightly back in the jungle when Barrel emitted his acidic breath. While all of them received injuries from stray drops that spattered through the foliage, no one was mortally injured.

When the moment came, Karlo was filled with hate for the kidnapping reptile and unleashed his arrow. It made contact perfectly with his chosen mark. Then Ragnar rushed forward screaming a bloodcurdling battle cry, and the deed was done. The dragon was dead, and his head and toe lay a few feet from the rest of his body.

Karlo rushed from cover and saw where Kerr lay in the dirt. He ran to check him out, his heart beating wildly in his chest. Kerr's right arm was totally gone, but his heart still beat feebly within his breast. Perhaps with love and tender care, Kerr might someday recover.

Barry emerged from the jungle, seeing Karlo occupied with Kerr, and turned to Ragnar. "Well, my heroic friend, you appear to have accomplished all we could hope for. The lich, the frost giant, and this dragon are all no more. No doubt with the destruction of the stone, the Queen's sanity has returned. You, Ahmad, the gryffons, the little scarab, and all those who shared this adventure with you will long live in the stories and songs of the people you have saved. But what is next for you?"

40

Twilight Breeze

by
Lynette White

Kerr's breathing was becoming erratic, and Karlo pulled him close.

"No, Kerr. Please hang on." Karlo pleaded.

The scarab cautiously crawled out Kerr's pocket, and Karlo grabbed it. "Where were you when he needed you?" He screamed and closed his hand.

In his blind rage and sorrow, Karlo had every intention of squeezing the life out of the beetle, but the scarab had different intentions. Karlo yelped in pain from the sharp shock emitted by the beetle and tossed it away from him.

The scarab scurried up to Kerr's shoulder and started its clicking sound. It settled on the damaged tissue and began to glow a soft gold. They gasped collectively as they witnessed the tissue begin to heal right where he stood.

The crystal sword on Ragnar's hip was growing warm and glowing the same color gold as the beetle.

"Is it possible?" Ragnar mused as he looked from the sword to the scarab. He could feel the sword starting to strum in urgency and pulled it from the scabbard.

The beetle stopped, jumped down, and turned its attention to Ragnar. The clicking sound it was making matched the strumming of the sword beat for beat.

"Blessed Odin." Ragnar muttered and walked toward the weeping Karlo.

He knelt down next to Kerr. "Hold him steady, Karlo, I think I can fix this."

Ragnar held his breath as he touched the tip of the sword to Kerr's shoulder and positioned it to be in the same alignment as a normal arm. The same soft colored light flowed from the sword and surrounded Kerr. The party watched in utter disbelief as the skin, tissue, and bone stretched until it ended just short of creating an elbow. The golden light subsided, and the new stump was a rosy pink. The color returned to Kerr's face and his breathing stabilized.

"In all my days… " Karlo whispered as the light faded, and the scarab quieted.

Kerr suddenly gasped for air.

Karlo pulled him close. "Quiet, young one. It is all right now. We are all here. It is all right now." Karlo comforted him.

Opening his eyes, Kerr stared at his partial arm in shock. The memory of the pain flashed as he looked up at his beloved uncle. "How?"

"The sword." Karlo smiled at Ragnar then touched the stump. "I am so sorry, Kerr."

Kerr gently rotated his shoulder. "The sword did this?" He whispered then smiled. "I will be all right, Uncle, and my what a story I will have to tell now."

Kerr looked directly at Ragnar. "Thank you, my friend. And the dragon?"

"… is dead." Ragnar quickly assured him.

Kerr managed a weak smile. "That is good, but his minions

will return as soon they discover I lied to them."

"Lied to them about what, Kerr?" Ragnar pushed.

"About where the eggs are hidden. I sent them the wrong way to give you time. I knew you would come for me." Kerr explained and closed his eyes. He was too weak and exhausted to keep them open.

Karlo pulled him into a tight embrace and tears of pride flowed down his gruff cheeks. "Kerr, my brave but foolish little warrior."

Ragnar stood up and wiped away tears of his own. He reached into his pouch and retrieved the red streaked egg. The words of warning from the Marine Toads echoed in his tired mind. He turned the egg to the words. "Darustrix Irthos: Levethix. Is that supposed to be your name? Levethix?"

They watched Ragnar place the egg down on the ground.

"Well, Levethix, I am afraid that is just not going to happen." He announced and replaced the crystal sword with his axe. "This is for what happened to Kerr." And with that the axe rended the egg in two.

Foul smelling acid from inside the egg forced Ragnar back. He covered his mouth and nose with his sleeve until the odor dissipated. A movement drew him back to the egg. Writhing on the ground was the most abominable thing he had ever seen. It was a dragon with arms and legs that were almost human but more closely resembled Calyptro. He flipped the axe and smashed the foul creature with the flat side until it stopped moving. Then for good measure, he chopped it in half.

The others slowly gathered around and gawked at Ragnar's handy work. Karlo helped Kerr to his feet. As Karlo looked down on the creature, he made a decision and moved away from the others. He walked outside and toward the dead dragon, Barrel the Terrible.

The others followed him. The foul acid was gathered in pools around the dead dragon, and Karlo walked around the corpse until he found a good-sized pool. He reached into his pocket and retrieved the necklace.

He tossed it into the acid, and a horrible screaming black mist rose up as Barrel's fluids ate at the fine metal and stones. They silently watched the necklace melt into a black lump of metal, and the gems were grossly discolored.

"You just reaped your final reward, Traven the Fallen. Evil will always destroy itself." Karlo declared.

"Let it be so," Kerr said. Jesper and Barry nodded in agreement.

"Blessed be to Odin." Ragnar added.

The sound of wings drew all eyes upward. Circling above them was Ahmad and the Gryffon Warriors. Ahmad pointed a safe distance away. Ragnar nodded and led the party to join them.

Ahmad and Simurgh stood side, by side and the riders formed up behind them waiting for the party to clear the trees. Ragnar and Ahmad clasped forearms as they came together.

"Welcome back, my brother." Ragnar greeted him.

"Welcome back yourself. There are some people who have been anxiously waiting to meet you." Ahmad greeted him in return and turned toward the men behind him. "Gentlemen, may I introduce you to Ragnar Olafson, the Gryffon Master's living heir."

Images of a similar scene played out by an ancient ancestor came unbidden to Ragnar's mind as each man dropped to one knee and lowered his head in respect.

A low whistle escaped Karlo's lips. "Will you look at that? The mighty gryffon warriors bow to no one. Have you ever seen anything so magnificent as the Gryffon Riders?"

"Except to the heir of a true Gryffon Master. There are no words to describe something like this," Ahmad interjected.

Ragnar glanced from Karlo to Ahmad. Simurgh stood up first and moved toward them.

"Simurgh, this is the Northman I have been telling you about." Ahamad explained. "Ragnar, this is Simurgh Bergstom. Gryffon Master until you returned."

"And still is as far as I am concerned." Ragnar remarked and extended his hand. "It is a pleasure to meet you."

Simurgh clasped forearms. "No, the pleasure is all mine as it is my pleasure to take you before the King. He is anxiously waiting to meet you and your party as well."

Ragnar broke his hold and looked at his ragtag party of warriors. They were filthy dirty, their clothes were torn, and they were so exhausted they could barely stand. Never in his dreams did he ever imagine such a mismatched bunch of warriors, but he would give his life for any one of them. "We are in no condition to stand before a king, Simurgh."

Simurgh laughed. "I think he will wait until you have cleaned up a little. Come, my riders will carry you to the camp."

Kerr perked up. "You mean I will be allowed to ride a mighty gryffon?"

Karlo scowled at him for being disrespectful, but Simurgh smiled down on the young dvergr. "Are you brave enough?"

Ragnar placed a gentle hand on Kerr's good shoulder. "Simurgh, this young man's name is Kerr, and he is the most dedicated, determined, and bravest warrior I have ever had the pleasure to stand beside in battle."

***

As Ragnar relaxed in the hot bath water, he realized how

badly he just wanted a good night's sleep. Now that this nightmare was finally over, he just might get that, then he would destroy the other eggs and find a way home.

After their baths they were given hot food, clean clothes, and a short time to rest. The sun was waning by the time Ragnar led his band of warriors into the King's tent. While they waited to be announced, his mind slipped to Woldar. He rubbed his clean-shaven face as he made a mental note to ask Simurgh to help him keep that promise.

"What are you thinking about, my friend?" Ahmad asked.

Ragnar dropped his hand and sighed. "A few things actually—a good night's sleep for starters. We still have three dragon eggs to find and destroy. And I have a promise to keep to one other outsider I found in the jungle. I promised him I would come back for him, and together we would find some way to get us all home again. Do you think Simurgh would consider helping me keep that promise?"

Ahmad looked down at his feet. "Was he about your size, human like us, dark hair, dressed in green?"

"Yes," Ragnar answered hesitantly. "His name is Woldar."

"I never knew what his name was." Ahmad said in a near whisper and looked back up at Ragnar. "I am afraid that is a promise you will not be able to keep, Ragnar. Simurgh and I found his body. We buried him in the jungle after we battled the frost giant. I am so sorry, my friend."

Ragnar looked away and wiped away a tear. He could not begin to count how many promises were broken because of death's touch.

The flap between them and the King's Court separated and a guard stepped out. "His Majesty will see you now."

Ragnar and Ahmad led the odd group of warriors inside. Sitting on a makeshift throne of pillows was the king and on a separate group was the most beautiful woman Ragnar had ever seen.

Ahmad's eyes locked on the woman. "Faella." He whispered.

"You know her?"

"Yes, Rostok took me to her when I left you." Ahmad quickly explained.

Ragnar rolled his eyes. "Figures! While I was digging through tombs, you were lying around with her."

"That is not exactly how it happened, Ragnar." Ahmad defended himself. "She rules over the Light Elementals."

"The Light Elementals?" Ragnar repeated and his memory flashed to the words written on the side of the cavern wall.

They stopped at the feet of the king, dropped to one knee and lowered their heads. Not quite the warriors the king was expecting. "So these are the heroes we owe our salvation to?" The king quickly regrouped. "Arise brave warriors and introduce yourselves."

Ragnar stood up first. "I am Ragnar Olafson from a land far distant.

Ahmad stood up next. "I am Ahmad Ibn Fazzat, also from a land far distant."

Karlo stood next and helped Kerr to his feet. "I am Karlo, son of Reginn, tribe of Valinn." Karlo introduced himself and pointed at Kerr. "This is my Tyro, Kerr, also from the Valinn tribe."

The others stood up and introduced themselves in turn.

"I am Calyptro."

"I am Barry."

"I am Jesper from the tribe of Leventrow."

The king turned to three servants on his left and motioned for them to step forward. "These medals are the first gifts of gratitude to be bestowed upon each of you for your service to the crown. Your bravery and courage will be documented and forever stored in the Kingdom Archives."

He motioned to the servants, and one by one they placed the medals over the heads of the heroes. When they finished and stepped back, the king spoke again.

"I am anxious to hear each of your stories, but since I wish to have them recorded, I will wait until tomorrow when we hold the feast in your honor. You will entertain us with your tales as we eat fine food and celebrate your victory."

Faella leaned closer to the king. "With your permission, Your Majesty, I wish to speak to Ragnar and Ahmad alone."

"Of course, Faella." He nodded and dismissed them with a wave of his hand.

She stepped down and took each of them by the arm. "Come with me, please?"

She quickly led them out of the king's tent and into her own. Ragnar was suspicious, but Ahmad seemed to trust her, so the Northman relaxed slightly.

"Please forgive my abruptness, but I wanted to discuss your options before decisions were made I could not stop. The King desires to keep you around for awhile longer." She apologized.

Now Ragnar was back on full alert. "What options?"

"Ragnar the Brave, what is your one desire?"

He was taken aback. "What?"

"What do you desire more than anything at this moment, Ragnar Olafson?"

He took a few moments to choose his answer. "To go home."

"I thought that would be your answer." She smiled and moved to Ahmad. "And what about you, Ahmad Ibn Fazzat? Do you wish to go home as well?"

Ahmad gulped. "Yes."

"Then this will be the only chance I have to help you accomplish that. But before I do I want you to understand how you came to be here." She started to explain.

Before their eyes she transformed, and Ragnar gasped as the woman who pleaded for his help appeared before him. He rushed off to help her and woke up in this strange land.

She transformed again and a young dark skinned woman appeared. This time Ahmad sucked in his breath. It was the same woman who lured him out of his tent for a walk in the moonlight.

She returned to her true form. "Now you understand?"

They both nodded dumbly. She looked down with shameful eyes. "If I had any other choice, I would have never done what I did to you but you were our only hope. I am so sorry, but now that we are safe again, I will help you get home."

Ragnar's mind slipped once again to Karagon, and his tale carefully written on a cavern wall. One hand went to the summoning stone and the other to the crystal sword. He did not notice until now that they softly strummed in perfect harmony.

"I saw a tale written about Traven the Fallen and the weapons—these weapons —created by the Light Elementals to stop him."

He reached into his shirt and pulled the summoning stone free. He then loosened the belt holding the crystal sword and offered them to Faella. "Please allow me to return them in gratitude for your help to get me home."

She took them from Ragnar and placed them on the pillows behind her. "Thank you, brave Ragnar. Allow me to reward you as well. Give me your Champion Axe, please."

Ragnar hesitated for a moment before reaching for his axe.

But then he cautiously presented it to her. She took a step back, tightened her hold on the heavy weapon, and started to chant. A golden light gathered around her then slowly encircled the axe. Both men stood transfixed as the axe transformed before their eyes. The light slowly dimmed, and she fell silent. She smiled at the stunned Ragnar, stepped forward, and she held out his axe.

He slowly lifted his hand and reclaimed his prized weapon. The blade glistened as if it had never touched an enemy. The handle from the knob to the belly was ivory, and the metal was unlike anything he had ever seen. It was lighter in weight but still perfectly balanced. Right at the edge of the ivory were three stones identical in shape, size, and arrangement to those on the crystal sword. Never in his life had Ragnar seen such an elegant weapon, much less imagined he would ever possess one.

"This blade will always protect you and never lose its edge as long as you wield it in righteousness, Ragnar."

"Thank you." He said and suddenly remembered the armor.

He started to reach for the straps to loosen it. But she shook her head. "No, take that as a gift as it was made especially for you."

She turned around and reached under the pillows. She grabbed an exquisite rapier, the weapon of choice for the warriors from Damascus, and presented it to Ahmad. The same ivory grip and gems adorned this elegant weapon.

"This is for you. Use this weapon wisely, and it will do the same for you as Ragnar's axe."

He took the weapon from her and bowed his head. "Thank you, but I am not a warrior."

She gently touched his face. "Ahh, but you are, Ahmad Ibn Fazzat." She corrected him and dropped her hand.

She turned away from them and started to chant once again.

The air shimmered, and a warm gentle breeze softly blew around them. She turned back to them and pointed at Ahmad. "This portal is known as the Twilight Breeze, and it will take you two home. You will feel a little disoriented at first, but it will be nothing like before. You first, Ahmad."

Ahmad paused and looked at Ragnar. The big Northman pulled him close, then pushed him away. "Go home to your destiny, Ahmad. I will never forget you."

"Nor I you." Ahmad said and stepped through the portal.

The warm desert air greeted him as he stepped through the portal just outside the main camp. Ahmad closed his eyes to keep everything from spinning. Once his world stabilized, he made his way toward camp, and he received a hero's welcome.

The breeze subsided the moment Ahmad stepped through the portal, but Faella repeated the words and turned to Ragnar.

"Now you."

He thought of Kerr and the others. "But I want to tell my companions goodbye first. After everything we have been through, I cannot leave them like this. We still have to destroy the eggs." He started to protest.

She shook her head knowingly. "No, Ragnar. It is better this way. When I tell them you have gone home, they will understand. They will stay in the King's service for a time and live rich lives as heroes. They will tell your story tomorrow at the feast, and I will see to it that Ahmad's story is told as well. You two will be revered here just as your forefathers were. The Gryffon Master made the decision to stay for a short time but never left this land. I do not want to see the same thing happen to you."

"As for the eggs, they have already been gathered up and taken to a safe place until they hatch."

"But..."

"Balance must be restored. Three were taken, three will take their place." She cut him off. "Barrel and the others fell victim to Traven's lies and paid the consequence. The young ones will take their rightful place in time as even evil has its place in the cycle, Ragnar."

She pointed at the portal. "Time to go home and fulfill your destiny as well, Ragnar Olafson."

Ragnar took a step toward the portal, but a movement in the pillows and a familiar clicking sound stopped him.

"The scarab?"

Faella gently shook her head. "No. It is his mate. They serve me when I require it. She knows her mate has returned, but she is agitated because he is reluctant to leave Kerr. It is something I will sort out later."

Ragnar chuckled. "Little Kerr does grow on you."

"Indeed he does." She agreed and nodded at the portal.

Ragnar shook his head and stepped toward the Twilight Breeze. The blast of cold air and the spinning sensation disoriented him.

He looked around and smiled. He was standing right outside his village gatehouse.

"Who goes there?" A gruff voice called out from the gatehouse.

Smiling, Ragnar recognized a familiar voice. "Arric, it is me, Ragnar Olafson. I have just returned from an amazing journey."

"Ragnar? Blessed Odin," Arric called back. There was a scuffling of feet in the gatehouse. A cheer echoed off the walls of the tower, and three men rushed down the steps.

"Find Lagertha, quick. Tell her there is no need to morn any longer."

Arric ordered one of the assistants, and the young man rushed off into the village.

AFTERWORD

by

Christian Warren Freed

When I was approached to participate in this story, I had trepidations to say the least. Working with different authors sounded fine, but the lack of creative control over how the story developed seemed alien. It takes a measure of swallowing your pride to get involved, which I believe all of the authors successfully did in order to create an engaging story. I volunteered to lead off. The inspiration came quickly. I borrowed the basic concept from Robert Rodriguez's Predators movie and had the two main characters wake up in an alien jungle. One Viking, one Arab, I drew on Michael Crichton's Eaters of the Dead (Later made into the 13th Warrior movie) and let the adventure begin. Much of the enjoyment of this story was reacting/anticipating the unexpected twists the other authors threw into the mix. The end result is something we can all be proud of. Hopefully you will enjoy too.

AFTERWORD
by
Joyce Shaughnessy

My writing background was historical fiction prior to 2013, but I was encouraged to try something new by members of my local writing group. I first wrote a fantasy short story in a LinkedIn Fiction Guild writers group started by H.M. Schuldt, and I was hooked. When Heather asked who might be interested in a round robin novel, I jumped at the chance. I admire Heather for her talented writing as well as her ability to organize and encourage other writers.

The concept of round robin novels was completely new to me as well as fantasy. I had never even read much fantasy before working on this novel, and I feel incredibly lucky to have worked on the book with Heather, Christian, Lynette, and Randall. They are four very gifted authors. We have worked well together, always courteous and respectful of each other, and as a result, the book flows as if it could have been written by one author. Because of the background and expertise of the others, I have learned an enormous amount about writing in general but especially fantasy.

I am excited about the release of this book because I think the reader will be constantly intrigued and surprised. When five different authors are allowed to work on the same project, the result is a wonderful book. The protagonists, Ragnar and Ahmad, are carefully built, and the book is replete with beautiful imagery as well as challenges for the main characters to overcome.

I will forever be grateful that I was lucky enough to be grouped with such talented writers. I have learned a great deal from them and consider them friends as well as colleagues.

GRYFFON MASTER

AFTERWORD

by

H. M. Schuldt

Gryffon Master is one of the most popular ancient stories found in jungles around the world. When I took a stroll through my local library, I was shocked to discover that no one has yet written this story. It was with great excitement that I called upon four writer friends to meet with me to explore details on this matter. Together we agreed to make this legendary story available, telling it just as it happened a long time ago, even though frost giants do not approve.

A friendly giant, Big Pine, told me that there are, still to this day, frost giants who regret not being able to capture the crystal sword. I was pleased to find out that these frost giants live at the North Pole, and they have no interest in returning to our world. When I told Big Pine we could make *Gryffon Master* available in a book, he was rendered temporarily speechless, choked up with emotion, and shed big tears when he said, "It is my wildest dream to tell the world about this Viking and Arab. Raganr and Ahmad have saved a jungle from great danger and from chaotic magic of necromancy. Their descendants have returned from time to time to make sure all is well."

The story of *Gryffon Master* unites all types of people, bringing us together to stand against slimy kings and skeletal creatures that hate the living world. Without any further ado, I invite you to see how Ragnar and Ahmad join together to stop hollow-eyed liches from destroying the jungle. You will find out how these two warriors, a Gryffon Master and a Sword Master, stop the gruesome undead from fighting against the living world.

AFTERWORD

by

Randall Lemon

When H.M. Schuldt first proposed the idea of a round robin novel, I was immediately intrigued. I had begun to work on my first fantasy novel and even though I had created almost 600 pages of source material from which to work, I had begun to find the process of creating the novel tedious. I had decided to take a breather by writing some short stories and flash fiction and had come across a site devoted to the creation of flash fiction pieces: Writers 750. Here Heather sponsors a writing contest each month for pieces from 750–1000 words long. She provides a theme, a setting, and three elements to be included in each story. It was great fun and supported by a group of extremely talented authors.

After a few months, Heather brought up the idea of a round robin novel and asked who might be interested. Two groups immediately formed. I jumped at the chance to join the Twilight Breeze group attempting to create a fantasy novel. Twice before I had worked on projects with co-authors and always found it challenging and stimulating. I thought it would be great fun to get involved and it became even more fun when I found out who my co-authors would be. I come from a fantasy background having been a longtime roleplaying gamer and was a great fan of heroic fantasy like the works of Robert E. Howard and his iconic hero, Conan the Barbarian. When it became apparent that our heroes would be two men brought from greatly disparate environments to yet a third environment with which neither was familiar, I was hooked. What could be more inspiring than a Viking warrior from the great white North joining a crafty Arab warrior to save the people of a jungle world? I hope you find the result as exciting as I did.

AFTERWORD
by
Lynette White

Doing a collaborative story was something I had never pictured myself ever doing. When I was asked to participate, I accepted it as a new challenge, and a challenge is exactly what it was. I am very particular about my stories, and so to let go and allow others to dictate the direction of my story was very difficult for me. However, this group brought some amazing talent to the table, and though we had a few hiccups along the way, I am proud of what we accomplished. As each author added their own flavor to the story, the twists and turns fell into place. You will find that each of us has our own distinct form of writing, but that does not mean it will be easy to put the book down. The adventures of Ragnar and Ahmad are perilous. Two strangers thrust into a strange land to fulfill a prophecy they had no idea existed. They become unwilling heroes in a battle they don't understand until its final moments.

We all face battles we don't understand, but still we fight on. You don't have to be in battle armor to go to war. You might be in a pair of jeans, a suit, a dress, a pair of gym shorts, or a military uniform, but still you fight for what you believe in. This story is dedicated to the warrior spirit in all of us.

Glossary

Glossary

Abdullah bin Khaleel ur Rahman - a Sand Skimmer Captain who helps Ahmad

Ahmad Ibn Fazzat – has a riding cloak; takes the crystal sword, takes two dragon claws, a fierce warrior

Ahrns the Troll – Arns Ska Kae Tung, Shaman of a swamp troll tribe is helpful to Ragnar; he tells Ragnar to destroy the necklace, he gives Ragnar a map to find the summoning stone that will bring Ahmad back

Ahrns's Map – located in a cave ten miles away from Arns the troll, it shows a "perfect triangle" locations between the sword, the necklace, and the summoning stone

Armor – (Adamantine Chain Mail) – Horgoth makes this for Ragnar; it is fireproof

Blessed of Bahamut – a desert ship (sand skimmer) with gold adornments and a golden dragonhead, the "Blessed of Bahamut" whose captain is Abdullah

Barrel the Terrible – an evil dark dragon; Ragnar's father warns Ragnar about this horrible dragon

Broken Arrow – a certain type of arrow, valuable, good for trading it at the Armor Hut for one set of fireproof armor; a talisman

Calyptro - the scout goblin; he knows this jungle like the back of his lizard hand

Candle Magic – Ragnar receives this from Roland; it transforms the glen by making a hut appear

Capin – friendly monkey pet belonging to Roland; white face, brown body, fetches fruit and nuts

Claws – two dark dragon claws are cut by Ahmad, one for Ahmad, one for Ragnar; one claw cuts Ahmad 's leg

Crow – symbol of the great solar god, Godlug; it shows Ahmad which path to take

Crystal Sword – has jewels similar to the jewels on the golden necklace; it has powers and can glow; it provides Ahmad a waterfall and sends Ahmad Rostok the gryffon

Djinn – various figures; some are in black with blue fire in his hand; other djinns include Reptile Djinns and Djinn Vultures

Dwarf Mine of Davlin – place where Karlo was trained

Faella – light elemental, a slender female, golden skin, long blond hair, appears to Ahmad, she tells Ahmad about *a curse that makes her land suffer*; she gives Ahmad a potion to give him strength when his courage fails

Giant Dragonfly – seen by Ragnar in a vision; it places a silvery item in a tree, which is stolen by a dragon

Gold Dragon – has a bountiful heart, sapphire eyes, cannot speak, dull in color, 50 meters from nose to tail; Ahmad heals its wound

Golden Necklace – stolen from a boneyard, three gems of ruby, sapphire, and emerald; one gem is the soul gem that gives a lich more time to exist

Gryffon Master – long ago, he destroyed the physical body of the evil sorcerer who traps souls; but he failed to destroy the necklace and the evil sorcerer's soul

Gryffon Warriors – ten fake warriors try to trick Ragnar; sent by Queen Valona to steal the necklace; defeated by the scarab beetle

Guss the Courier – jolly little goblin messenger for Roland; brings Roland a broken arrow and news about the kidnapped jeweler, Jesper

Horgoth Anvilstriker – a smithy dvergr who lives in a magical glen; Queen Valona's brother, exiled by Valona since he spoke against her; he wants his sister's sanity back

Hygliak the Goblin – a small green goblin; has a child-like voice, batwing ears, small eyes, patches of grey-green hair, smells bad, saves Ahmad and Rostok from the Djinn; he is a scout from the king's army

Jesper – a good dvergr jeweler kidnapped by a boneman

Jotun – frost giants from Jotunheimr; has a foreign scream, ground trembles when he steps

Karlo – a tall dvergr, son of Reginn from the tribe of Valinn, black hair, Uncle to Kerr

Kerr – pale skinned dvergr, black hair; nephew to Karlo; Karlo's apprentice

King Andren – husband to the crazy Queen Valona; he has Karlo take the necklace away to get rid of it; he likes to drink spiced grog

Lagertha – Ragnar's wife, a shieldmaiden, fights beside Ragnar in previous times

Leather clothes – given to Ragnar by Horgoth, to replace Ragnar's furry clothes

Match Magic – Horgoth uses this to transform his fireplace into a huge "forge"

Prophecy – two men shall come to save the land from a terrible curse of the Lich King, one man shall be a pale skinned fierce warrior while the other man shall be a dedicated soldier with sun-darkened skin; the two men will end the curse of the lich king

Queen Valona – obsessed with getting the gold necklace back; her husband sends Karlo to take the necklace away

Rachelle Trevlin – a "lost princess" arrives on a gryffon pretending to help Ragnar; she brings "ten gryffon warriors" and a human-tree to distract Ragnar; she tries to send Ragnar to "the library"

Ragnar Olafson the Northman – pale skin, blond hair, animal skin clothes, tattoo on face and arms, comes from tall mountains, battleaxe "Mastare" means champion, a son of Odin, descendant of a Gryffon Master, his wife is Lagertha

Ratatoskr the Squirrel – has horns; tells Ragnar "a lich is upon you; he will transport you to the world of Nodhogrr"

Regal Scarab Beetle – almost as big as Kerr's palm; same size and color as Ragnar's summoning stone; a wizard, it dispenses justice when malevolence is discovered

Roland the Troll – helps Ragnar; lives in a hut, gnarled hands, bent back, old, strange; has power to see into the future and the past

Rosy Periwinkle – special petals make a powerful tonic to give Karlo and Kerr strength

Sand Skimmer – a desert ship (see Bahamut)

Sanyogita - the City in the Sand – a place where the Festival of Youth is celebrated; camel races are held here, near the Temple of Life

Sea of Sand – Faella sends Ahmad on a quest to this location where two dragons battle and Ahmad collects two dragon claws

Simurgh – a Persian man who rides on his gryffon, Rostok; he allows Ahmad to borrow his gryffon

Skull Dragon - a horrible black dragon used by liches and djinns; emits fire and poisonous miasma

Skyrim the frost giant – Karlo defeats this frost giant with Ragnar's arrow dipped in scorpion poison; it retreats into the trees

Vatman – a lich from the Sunken Tomb of Vatomandry; he wants the necklace back, an undead sorcerer, he wants to prolong his undead existence

Woldar the Woodsman – the third human

Yggdrasil Tree – a magical tree tall enough to disappear into the heavens

PROFESSOR K.R. LIMN BOOKS

GIANT TALES:
Beyond the MYSTIC DOORS
From the MISTY SWAMP
World of Pirates
LAVA STORM

CRYSTAL SWORD CHRONICLES:
GRYFFON MASTER

www.ingramcontent.com/pod-product-compliance
Lightning Source LLC
Chambersburg PA
CBHW022145240626
47153CB00007B/2510